THE MINSTREL'S MALADY

Sandal Castle Medieval Thrillers

Book Five

Keith Moray

THE MINSTREL'S MALADY

Published by Sapere Books.

24 Trafalgar Road, Ilkley, LS29 8HH

saperebooks.com

ISBN: 978-0-85495-263-2

Keith Moray is represented by Isabel Atherton at Creative
Authors.

For Florence, who knows and loves Cawthorne.

There was not a minstrel in all the land
Who could offer any entertainment
Who did not flock to the court.
Great was the joy in the hall:
Each performed his service:
One leaps, one tumbles, one conjures,
One tells tales, the other sings,
One whistles, the other plays tunes,
This one plays the harp, this the rote,
This the gigue, this the fiddle,
This the flute and this the shawm.
Maidens carol and dance.
All strive to make joy.

Erec et Enide, *Arthurian Romances*
Chrétien de Troyes (1130–1190)

LIGHTBORN:
You shall not need to give instructions;
'Tis not the first time I have killed a man;
I learned in Naples how to poison flowers,
To strangle with a lawn thrust through the throat,
To pierce the wind-pipe with a needle's point,
Or whilst one is asleep, to take the quill
And blow a little powder in his ears,
Or open his mouth and pour quicksilver down,
But yet I have a braver way than these.

MORTIMER:
What's that?

LIGHTBORN:
Nay, you shall pardon me, none shall know my tricks.

Edward II, **Act V, Scene IV**
Christopher Marlowe (1564–1593)

But there is no bodily infirmity, not even leprosy or epilepsy, which cannot be caused by demons or witches, with God's permission.

**Malleus Maleficarum, '*Hammer of Witches*', 1487
Heinrich Kramer (*Henricus Institor*) (1430–1505)**

PROLOGUE

Hereford Castle, 17 November 1326

The three prisoners had been unceremoniously lowered into the oubliette, the bottle-neck dungeon cell that had been hewn from the bedrock. There was no light apart from the flickering of a single guttering candle in an iron sconce above the grille that was the roof of the oubliette. From time to time they heard the shuffle of the guards, the rattle of keys, or the bored unmelodic song of their jailors.

'How are your hands, my Lord Arundel?' asked one of the three.

'They pain me, Sir Thomas, which is exactly as that bastard de Charlton intended when he had his men break my fingers.'

Thomas de Micheldever, the clerk to Edmund Fitzalan, the Earl of Arundel winced as he tried to push himself up on his elbows, his fingers having suffered the same injuries as his lord. 'I can still hear the snapping of the bones, my lord.'

'And what of your mouth, Sir John?' the earl asked.

Sir John Daniel groaned. 'It hurts greatly, my lord. I can feel the broken teeth every time I move my tongue and I taste the blood. Being punched by Sir John de Charlton's steel gauntlet is not something I would care to feel again, although I would give anything to return the compliment someday.'

The three men at the head of a small party had been on their way to Shropshire the day before. They had left King Edward II and his chamberlain and favourite, Hugh le Despenser, at Cardiff after they had tried to sail to Lundy Island en route to Ireland to raise an army against Queen Isabella, the king's wife, and her lover Sir Roger Mortimer, the Earl of March. Ever loyal to King Edward, Edmund in his capacity as Warden of the Welsh Marches and the Chief Justiciar of North and South Wales had been despatched to array troops to protect the king. It was a bitter blow when, outside Shrewsbury, they had run into his arch enemy Sir John de Charlton, whom he had supplanted as the Warden of the Marches the year before, and from whom he had taken lands and manors. After a brief skirmish, Edmund's party was overcome and he, Sir John Daniel and Sir Thomas de Micheldever were beaten and abused.

Sir John de Charlton took pleasure in having the Earl of Arundel at his mercy. 'You thieving mongrel and lickspittle to that fiend who claims the throne and his creature le Despenser: those fingers of yours will do no more grasping of my lands and titles.'

He ordered his men to throw Edmund down upon the ground and break his fingers one by one.

When Thomas de Micheldever tried to intervene, he too was thrown down.

'And you can share your master's punishment!' cried de Charlton.

'You cowardly dog!' roared Sir John Daniel. 'Why, I will —'

'You will speak only when I allow it,' de Charlton replied disdainfully, before punching him in the face, spraying broken teeth and blood. The knight was already being held by two soldiers and almost collapsed from the force of the blow, which snapped his head back.

Then all three were stripped, shackled, dressed in tabards and made to sit on asses that were used to carry water and food for the superior force. The rest of their party had their weapons and whatever protective clothes they had removed. These were then tied to their backs while they were made to walk all the way to Hereford.

As they approached the town, they were greeted by the noise of trumpets and cymbals, the townsfolk having been stirred up by advance riders who had carried the news to Queen Isabella, who was staying at Hereford Castle. The queen told them to announce to the people that Sir John de Charlton was coming with important prisoners, traitors to her son King Edward III, to the royal family and to the Lord Protector, Sir Roger Mortimer, the Earl of March.

The greeting the people gave was anything but welcoming. Rotten vegetables, offal, dung and stones were cast at the prisoners, and without their armour's protection, they received many blows to add to the injuries they had already received. If the Earl of Arundel had thought himself popular with the common people, he was brutally shown otherwise.

When they were dragged before Queen Isabella, she castigated them and ordered Sir John de Charlton to cast them into the deepest dungeon at the castle while she decided what punishment they would receive.

Edmund Fitzalan, the Earl of Arundel began to plead with her, but he was silenced immediately by a blow to his head that sent him into a swoon. His companions dared not protest. The earl was not aware of much else until he awoke in considerable pain in the dark, damp oubliette.

When the jailors came for them in the morning, all three were in a miserable state.

'Water, for pity's sake,' rasped Sir John Daniel.

'And some crusts of bread at least,' added Thomas de Micheldever.

The jailors said nothing, but manhandled them one by one, forcing them to climb the ladder that had been lowered from the guardroom above.

'Her Majesty the Queen demands your presence outside the castle,' said a captain of the guards once all three had been removed from the oubliette.

'Further humiliation, I warrant,' Edmund said softly to his companions. 'Hold your heads high and show them what stout Englishmen are made of.'

To their horror, once outside the castle they saw a braying crowd. They were shoved towards a makeshift wooden stage and forced to climb the steps. Once atop it they saw three great blocks of wood.

A priest stood with a Bible next to a huge man with bare arms and a leather mask over his face. His hands were resting on the handle of a great axe.

'Where is the queen?' the earl demanded. 'What is this?'

A courtier came up the steps behind them. 'Her Majesty awaits your heads,' he said, his voice dispassionate.

Edmund Fitzalan recognised the man only too well. It was Sir Jasper de Beausale, one of the knights who had been with his enemy Sir John de Charlton and who had taken pleasure in abusing him. Yet only a few months before, he had been one of the earl's vassals.

'But Sir Jasper, you know me. I am the Earl of Arundel. I am a cousin to Sir Roger Mortimer himself. He —'

'You are a traitor! You are all traitors,' came the reply, cutting him off.

'W-we have had no trial,' stammered the earl. 'This cannot be… I demand…'

'The order has been given by Queen Isabella herself,' replied Sir Jasper de Beausale. Ignoring further protestations from Sir John Daniel and Thomas de Micheldever, he signalled for the priest to stand forth.

The terrified priest clutched his open Bible and avoided looking directly at the prisoners. He muttered some hasty words, closed his Bible and descended the steps as quickly as he could, as the crowd cursed and shouted at the three cowering men.

'Executioner, is your axe prepared as the Earl of March instructed?' Sir Jasper de Beausale demanded in a loud voice. 'Suitable for traitors to the king?'

The executioner's voice was muffled behind his mask. 'It is, sir. I have blunted it by cleaving a rock with it, as ordered.'

Sir Jasper turned to the crowd. 'The queen proclaims that all three of these traitors are arraigned; they forfeit titles, land and life. The first will be the one who was the Earl of Arundel, Edmund Fitzalan.'

Unable to believe what was about to happen, Edmund was forced to his knees and bent over one of the blocks of wood. He felt a foot push him down so that his neck rested in the hollow. Then a hand roughly shoved his hair up and he felt a breeze on his exposed neck.

The headsman raised his axe and struck. With the blunt axe it took five blows before the screaming stopped and in total some twenty blows before the earl's head was separated from his body.

Both Sir Thomas de Micheldever and Sir John Daniel had to be revived with buckets of water cast over them when their turn came for the axe.

The crowd's reactions were mixed. Some cried words of encouragement as the executioner carried out each blow, his strength visibly flagging by the time he was hacking at the third prisoner, spraying blood across the stage. Others sneered and laughed, while others looked away and prayed for it all to finish so that they could leave the scene.

Among the throng there was one who would have been known to all three of the condemned men, and quite possibly also to Sir Jasper de Beausale himself, were it not for the liripipe hood which hid his features. Powerless to do anything but watch, a silent oath was made. There would be retribution on all involved in this atrocity, even if it took a lifetime to achieve.

1

Cawthorne Priory, Yorkshire, 1329

Sister Odelina had been given the last rites and was declared dead to the world. Now two of the lay sisters, both weeping copiously, were sealing the mortar between the final stones of her cell, which had been built behind the high altar and was now to be her tomb for eternity.

Only, Sister Odelina was not dead.

Cawthorne Priory was one of the few houses of the Gilbertine Order, the only truly English order which permitted both monks and nuns to live and worship within the same community. The order had been founded by Saint Gilbert of Sempringham in Lincolnshire in 1130, who established eleven of these double houses throughout England before his death in 1190.

As with all Gilbertine communities there was a single church, which followed the usual liturgical layout, being built east to west, so that the end of the church with the altar was facing east. The unique feature was a wall that divided the church unequally, giving each side a transept and the building its traditional cross shape. The nuns had the larger part, and the monks the smaller. The nuns and monks would meet only to celebrate Mass together, although they would never see each other because of the dividing wall. It was designed so that there would be strict segregation of the sexes, apart from when the prior and the Mother Superior had to communicate, or when the prior or his deputy canons attended the nuns' side of the church to give communion and to hear their confessions.

Built into the dividing wall was the *fenestra versatilis*, a wooden turntable with four compartments so that sacred objects could be passed through the wall during worship without one side seeing the other. Into one of these compartments the two lay sisters placed their wooden buckets of mortar and the tools they had used to seal up the cell, so that lay brothers on the other side could remove and dispose of them.

The cell had been constructed behind the high altar to signify the order's reverence for the anchoress. It would not be overlong, they all believed, before Sister Odelina would be sainted.

The three nobles who had just arrived had been guided to chairs in the quire of the nave to watch at a distance the last part of the walling-in.

Standing immediately on the left of the altar was the Mother Superior, now joined by the two nuns. They watched as Prior Dominic splashed holy water from a small silver bowl on the wall and led the small assembly in prayer for Sister Odelina.

Mother Griselda looked round and bowed her head at the three nobles. 'May our distinguished guests talk to our blessed sister now, Father?' she asked.

Prior Dominic looked at her in alarm and then emphatically shook his head. 'No! Sister Odelina has chosen to become an anchoress of her own free will. It is fitting that she should be left to spend her first night in this cell that shall be her home until her mortal end and after that, her tomb. This is what we agreed before.'

'I just thought that, since we owe them so much…' Mother Griselda said in a low voice. 'Since they are here!'

Prior Dominic turned towards their guests and bowed. He walked to the *fenestra versatilis* and placed the bowl of holy water into a compartment, then spun the turntable to send it into the monks' presbytery.

Approaching them with his hands together and now hidden in his voluminous sleeves, he bowed again.

'I regret that it will not be possible to disturb Sister Odelina today. She has already bound a cloth around her mouth and another over her eyes and ears. It is her wish not to communicate with anyone except the Lord himself today.'

The three nobles muttered between themselves and then, with a nod at each other, the two males rose to their feet and held out hands for the lady.

She stared at them both coldly for a moment before accepting their hands and standing. Turning to face the Mother Superior and the prior, she sighed and shook her head.

'As you know, we three are not in the best of health, and each would wish to spend a few moments with Sister Odelina. She has helped us all with our ailments in the past and we believe that her touch alone —'

'The Anchoress Odelina will be able to pray for you as before. If you come tomorrow, you will be able to see her through the squint hole that we have left —'

He indicated two small holes which had been left in the wall. One was no more than a small cross-shaped peephole positioned less than five feet from the floor. The other was a circular opening on the floor, covered by a sliding metal grille no more than a handspan in diameter, which was not visible beyond the altar. It had been considered large enough to push through a small jug of water, some bread and perhaps some broth. It would also be large enough for the small chamber pot that would be emptied every day by one of the lay sisters, and for laundered clothes to be threaded through.

'An eye-hole?' said the taller of the two men. 'Prior Dominic, I can barely see this wall you say you have sealed the sister behind, let alone an eye-hole. Don't you know that sight is my very worst problem? And don't you understand that with the country in the state that it is in now, I must be able to see! Not to mention this infernal neck problem of mine.' He rubbed his neck and then twisted it to the side so that an obvious crunching noise could be heard. 'It has become so noticeable that people call me Wryneck behind my back.'

Prior Dominic was a good-looking man in his mid-forties, a few years older than the noble. He was clean-shaven and dark-haired, apart from his tonsure. He was too polite to comment on their afflictions. 'My apologies, my Lord Lancaster. It is in accordance with the ceremony of walling-in and with the wishes of the Anchoress Odelina herself.'

'You will all be most welcome to stay overnight,' Mother Griselda offered. 'Lady Isabella can stay in our guest house in the nunnery.'

'And my Lord Bishop of Durham and Lord Henry of Lancaster can stay in the hospitium in the monastery,' Prior Dominic was quick to add. 'Our brothers and sisters will arrange to make your stay comfortable. And we will be able to accommodate whatever retinue you have each brought with you.'

Lady Isabella de Vesci clicked her tongue and shook her head. 'I do not like the idea of Sister Odelina becoming an anchoress. Just how much space does she have in there? Is she in complete darkness?'

'She has adequate space, Lady Isabella,' said Mother Griselda. 'The anchoress cell occupies the whole of the chancel on this side of the dividing wall. There is a high window, so she will be able to see the sky and clouds during the day and the heavens and the stars at night.'

'But no trees, no animals?'

'There will be birds, bats and insects,' replied Mother Griselda. 'Whatever creatures the Lord permits. And there is a rod so that she can open and close the window for fresh air, as well as a shutter, should she wish to contemplate and pray in the dark. Or she can light her candles.'

Lady Isabella gave the Bishop of Durham, her brother, a sour look. 'Did you sanction this?'

Lewis de Beaumont, Bishop of Durham, stared back haughtily. 'It was not up to me, sister. Archbishop Melton and the Abbot of Sempringham, the head of the Gilbertine Order, allowed it. I have not seen Sister Odelina myself since the last time I was here. The last time we all met.'

'Nor have I, nor my Lord Lancaster,' Isabella de Vesci returned. 'And that time we agreed the course of action we should take after her message to us.' She turned sharply to give the prior and the Mother Superior a withering stare.

'And you both know the importance of the decision and the orders we three patrons of this priory gave that day!'

Prior Dominic and Mother Griselda both bowed their heads.

'We do, Lady Isabella, but this was Sister Odelina's decision,' said Mother Griselda.

Lady Isabella frowned. 'But why now, when we all have need of her help with our ailments? My brother because he is well-nigh crippled with his feet and has to be carried beyond twenty paces, my Lord Lancaster because he is going blind, and I because my joints are swelling and fail to bend as they should. She helped each of us with that birth gridle she wrapped round our ailing parts, but now you tell us that we can only see her through a squint hole?'

Mother Griselda smiled deferentially. 'It will still be possible to apply the birth girdle that she wore before her miracle occurred, my lady.'

'But will it work without her healing hands?' Lady Isabella de Vesci persisted. 'She is almost a saint, after all.'

Mother Griselda raised her hands as if to indicate that she did not know.

'Is there not also the relic of Saint Gilbert?' one of the sisters suggested.

Prior Dominic smiled at the young woman and nodded in agreement. 'Indeed, there is. I would be happy to make it available to those in need of the saint's healing.'

The three nobles muttered together, then Lady Isabella nodded. 'Very well, we shall all three stay this night and see Sister Odelina tomorrow — through this peephole! We shall see what she advises us each to do. But I have one question for you now. Why has she chosen to become an anchoress?'

Mother Griselda bit her lip. 'She … she said she did not feel safe in this world, my lady.'

The Mother Superior and the prior glanced nervously at each other. Prior Dominic turned to the two nuns. 'I think perhaps the sisters could await your attention outside.'

As the lay sisters took their leave, Prior Dominic attempted a reassuring smile.

'Sister Odelina wished to retire from the world, which she thinks to be an evil place. By devoting herself to the Lord and retreating, she felt she could do greater work. She can intercede for more souls in purgatory.'

'She has had more visions, hasn't she?' Lady Isabella said.

Prior Dominic bit his lip and nodded. 'She has, my lady.'

'Were they like the ones we all agreed we should act upon and inform — him?'

The prior nodded.

The bishop cut in. 'You sent the messenger, as we instructed?'

'We did, my Lord Bishop.'

'And the messenger knows that under no circumstances should the message be discovered to have come from here?'

'Indeed, Your Grace. They would perish first. By their own hand, if need be.'

'And have there been more deaths?' Lady Isabella asked.

'There have not been any more here, my lady,' Mother Griselda replied, crossing herself as she spoke. 'We are still grieving for our sisters and brothers whom the Lord took before their time.'

'And have there been other deaths … elsewhere?' Henry of Lancaster asked.

'Not that we are aware of, my lord,' Prior Dominic replied. 'But the visions were — disturbing. Sister Odelina has foreseen many deaths, destruction of all that has been built, and more treachery.'

'That is why our sister has taken this step, sacrificing herself to pray for us all,' Mother Griselda added, nodding at the wall behind which Sister Odelina had been imprisoned. She wiped away the tears that had run down her cheeks.

'And that is why she was adamant — she said it could mean her death if she is disturbed before she has finished praying and communicating with her angel.'

From behind the wall came the sound of a woman humming. It sent chills down Lady Isabella's spine.

She clutched the arms of the bishop and the Earl of Lancaster. 'I fear that we are undone.'

'No one is safe,' agreed the Bishop of Durham.

'They would be if I could see properly,' growled Lancaster. 'That is why I must be able to see again.'

Lady Isabella de Vesci shivered as she stared at the wall with its dark peephole. 'I'm beginning to think we all would be safer hidden behind a wall where we can pray until the mercy of death releases us to go to the Lord.'

2

Winchester, 12 March 1330

'What was he like, my lord, our new King Edward the Third?'

Sir Richard Lee yawned as he undid his belt and handed it together with his sheathed dagger to his servant, Hubert of Loxley. It was already dark outside and the low-ceilinged room was lit by three guttering candles.

'He resembles our late King Edward the Second, but he is seventeen years old and still beardless. He is as tall as myself and will probably grow to be as tall as his father, or perhaps even as tall as yourself, Hubert.'

Richard and Hubert were both in their thirties and had been through battle, hardship and many adventures together. Hubert had been a man-at-arms in the service of Sir Jasper Loxley, the father of Richard's first wife, Eleanor. After her death, Sir Richard answered his sovereign's call and fought against the Marcher Lords at Hereford, Pembroke and Shrewsbury. Later, they had been involved in the rout of Thomas, the Earl of Lancaster's army at Boroughbridge, as they tried to cross the River Ure. Richard had taken an arrow in his calf during the battle that went straight through the muscle and into the belly of his horse. It fell and had pinned him under it, leaving him at the mercy of a couple of Lancaster's infantrymen. Fortunately, Hubert was always at his side and outfought and dispatched them with his broadsword, saving his master's life. Afterwards Richard was taken to the Abbey of St Mary in York, where the poison on the arrow left him raving with fever for two weeks. All the while he was watched over by Hubert, who was distrustful of the potions the Benedictine monks there plied him with.

Upon his recovery Richard was ordered to attend upon His Majesty, King Edward II at York Castle. There he was given his special commission as Circuit Judge of the King's Northern Realm and Coroner to Wakefield and the five towns around. This effectively made him the Judge of the King's Bench in the North, with jurisdiction over the Manor of Wakefield and the Demesne of Pontefract.

Hubert lay Richard's belt and dagger on the wooden chest in the room in the Three Moons Tavern. He and Richard were staying there until after the parliament had convened and deliberated on the important matters of state. He smiled as he helped his master remove his surcoat.

'But though he is not yet of age to rule on his own, he has proven himself old enough to father a child,' Hubert said. 'I heard some of the servants at the castle say that it does not look to be long before Queen Philippa gives birth.'

'I did not see Her Majesty when I and the other sergeants-at-law and judges swore the oath of fealty before the king. We knelt before the throne and vowed to uphold the law in his name before kissing his ringed fingers. It was not up to us to speak, unless spoken to by His Majesty. Especially as Sir Roger Mortimer, the Earl of March was standing behind the throne, overseeing matters in his role as Lord Protector.'

He yawned again. 'We will sup and then I need to sleep well, as it has been a long day and I will have to be attentive tomorrow.'

Along with many of the sheriffs and judges in England, Sir Richard had been summoned again on the following morning to swear allegiance and vow to uphold the law of the land in

King Edward III's name. And then he was to attend at a parliament that Queen Isabella had called to be held at Winchester Castle, for he had been told that new laws were to be passed. He needed to hear what they were lest he had to implement them in his court.

'But you did talk to the king, my lord?' Hubert enquired eagerly.

'I did, but it was a mere few sentences. He knew of me and that I had been of some service to his father on several occasions. He said he would value the same support from me.'

Hubert chuckled. 'We — I mean you, of course, my lord — saved King Edward's life and that of one of his favourites.'

Richard handed Hubert his surcoat and shivered, for the room was cold and draughty. He accepted the woollen knee-length tunic in its stead. As he put it on he suppressed another shudder, not because of the cold this time, but because of an unwelcome memory. Although he had saved both the king and his favourite eight years before, he had been unable to prevent the late king's chamberlain, Hugh Despenser the Younger, from being hanged, drawn and quartered at Hereford in November 1326. His death followed a month after his father Hugh Despenser the Elder, the Earl of Winchester had been hanged in his armour, after which his body was cut up and fed to the dogs. As he looked out of the mullioned window of his room in the tavern, Richard could see the castle gate where the earl's head had been displayed on a spike.

'We live in strange and dangerous days, Hubert,' he suddenly mused.

'In what way, my lord?'

'I was just thinking of the fate of King Edward the Second's favourites. Piers Gaveston, the Earl of Cornwall was murdered and beheaded several years ago, then the Despensers four years ago. And now the very man who ordered their executions virtually oversees everything that happens throughout the land.'

'You mean Sir Roger Mortimer, my lord?'

'He has great influence over King Edward. He was actually sitting on the queen's throne next to King Edward. No one else would dare do that.'

'But as Queen Isabella's favourite, surely he is like the king's father?'

'The king did not look comfortable. Mortimer's men were in the Great Hall in force, all of them heavily armed.'

Hubert harrumphed. 'But surely the king has his own guards?'

'He had a group of his friends in the Great Hall, but they were only lightly armed with their daggers, like myself.' Richard frowned. 'I had not thought of it overmuch before, but when I received the summons to attend, the document said that swords were not to be worn in the castle. As a judge and lawyer I assumed it was protocol in front of the king. Yet clearly the king's contingent were similarly ordered, whereas Sir Roger Mortimer's men were not. They wore mail under their surcoats and they had swords.'

'Do the king's friends look like fighting men, my lord?'

Richard nodded. 'They are all knights and nobles, and most are a few years older than him. I have met Sir William de Montagu, who is a good knight and skilled in the joust. William de Bohun, William Clinton and John Neville are also good knights who I think would be dependable. Yet it troubles me that only Sir Roger Mortimer's men were permitted to wear arms.'

'Mayhap he fears for himself, my lord. We have all heard of his reputation and he is not a popular man — even if Queen Isabella, the king's mother, does seem besotted with him.'

With a sigh Hubert reached under his own tunic and drew out a chain that hung around his neck. An old arrowhead dangled from it.

'I wish I could persuade you to wear this wondrous arrowhead of mine, my lord,' he said.

Richard smiled. Hubert had bought the arrowhead in a tavern from a man who claimed to have been an old soldier. He had been told that it had been removed from the back of a crusader at the Battle of Antioch and that the crusader survived what should have been a mortal wound, and that ever afterwards he wore it for the rest of his long life and was never ill. Since then, Hubert had worn the arrowhead on a chain about his neck and was convinced that it had the power to protect him from illness and harm.

Richard patted his friend on the shoulder. 'You keep it, Hubert. I am happy knowing that you are safe.'

With a shrug Hubert tucked it back inside his tunic. 'In that case, my lord, don't go getting yourself in danger without me by your side.'

From cockcrow the following morning Winchester started to grow busy. Men on horseback, pony-drawn wagons and people herding animals or carrying wares filled the streets.

Sir Richard and Hubert made their way on foot from the Three Moons Tavern to the castle. It was the very first Norman castle in England, built by King William of Normandy, known to all as the Conqueror. He had it constructed on the elevated site of an earlier Roman fort, and upon a Saxon wooden palisade that succeeded it. It was essentially an oblong structure above the city, its eastern wall separating it from the buildings of the city by a huge ditch and mound. The surrounding stone wall with mighty towers concealed and protected the halls, chapels, gardens and the great stone keep that had housed the royal apartments, until a fire during Edward I's reign.

At the main twin-turreted gate they parted. Hubert went to visit the markets, while Sir Richard joined a stream of other dignitaries who were greeted by clerks and liveried servants and guided to the Great Hall.

Richard had been there the day before, when he had sworn his oath to King Edward. The king had sat at the end of the huge aisled hall and in front of the massive circular table of King Arthur, which hung high upon the wall under three brightly illuminated stained-glass windows. None could fail to be impressed by the grandeur of the Great Hall, nor the sight of the Round Table, knowing that at some time in the distant past the table had been upon the floor and that the great King Arthur and his worthy knights had sat around it, discussing laws and organising quests.

Shown to his seat in one of the aisles by one of the town burgesses, Richard found himself beside Sir Ranulf Fermont, who held a similar Manor Court near Lincoln. Richard had met Sir Ranulf many times and knew him to be a fair-minded and knowledgeable judge. He was somewhat deaf and applied a cow horn to his left ear, turning his head and directing the horn towards the person he wanted to hear. Richard was unsure how effective it was, since he tended to speak very loudly.

'I wonder how many laws Mortimer is going to impose on us today,' Sir Ranulf said, his voice carrying above the conversations around them as people continued to be shown to their seats.

Richard leaned towards the cow horn. 'I suggest you temper your words, Sir Ranulf,' he cautioned.

Sir Ranulf turned to stare at him and then nodded to indicate understanding that he may be seated near to others who were in thrall to Sir Roger. He nodded and then, leaning towards Richard, spoke in what was still a loud whisper. 'Best be careful, I know.'

Richard spoke into the horn again. 'I think we must be prepared for anything, Sir Ranulf.'

'Well, listen carefully, just in case I miss something.'

Richard gave the old judge a nod of assurance and returned his attention to those who were entering the hall. The seats towards the front, directly facing the raised dais and the two empty thrones below the Round Table, were now being taken up by the nobility of the realm: earls, dukes and lords, bishops and all of the Members of Parliament for the counties of England.

It was unusual for so many sergeants-at-law and judges to have been summoned to the parliament, and Richard assumed it was to swear allegiance to the new king and to hear first-hand about any new laws that were to be made. Over the last few years, many new laws had been added, then rescinded and further ones made in their place.

A trumpet sounded and the whole assembly scraped chairs on the floor as they stood, everyone looking round and getting ready to bow as royalty approached.

Yet to everyone's surprise there was no sign of King Edward. Instead, walking in front of a band of heavily armed guards, some with pikestaffs, Sir Roger Mortimer strutted regally down the central aisle, dressed in a black tunic that he had famously worn at the funeral of King Edward II at St Peter's Abbey of the Holy and Indivisible Trinity in Gloucester three years before.

'Where's the —?' Sir Ranulf blurted out, before he was silenced by Richard placing a finger to his lips.

The sudden silence of the assembly intensified the echoing of Mortimer's boots upon the floor as he strode to the dais, mounted it and took his seat not in the queen's place, but on King Edward's throne. His guards divided in two and went to stand to the right and left at the foot of the dais.

Ignoring the collective intake of breath around the Great Hall, Sir Roger surveyed the assembly for several moments before speaking from the throne.

'His Majesty the King cannot attend this parliament today and so I have full authority.'

A wave of restlessness spread across the Great Hall as people turned to one another.

'But there has been a change of plan, and the parliament will not take place this day.'

At this there were a few noisy outcries from the lords and the Members of Parliament.

Mortimer merely sat back with the ghost of a smile as he languidly stroked his neatly groomed beard with an elegant finger. After a few moments he signalled to a guard, who thumped the end of his pikestaff three times upon the floor. The noise reverberated through the Great Hall and the assembly immediately went silent.

Sir Roger Mortimer nodded and sat forward. 'You will note that there are several empty chairs in front of me. Edmund of Woodstock, the Earl of Kent and several of his adherents, including Lord Crispin of St Albans, are unable to attend.'

'Why, in God's name?' someone in the centre of the hall cried out.

Mortimer smiled and stood up, raising his chin as he tried to espy the caller.

'It is in God's name, sirrah,' he replied, raising his own voice. 'And also in the king's name. The Earl of Kent and his adherents have been arrested on a charge of high treason against King Edward.'

'But you can't do that!' another cried out. 'Sir Edmund is the king's uncle.'

'Aye, and he is the late King Edward's younger brother,' called yet another in agreement.

Mortimer raised his hands for silence. 'All you need to know is that he has been arrested and this assembly is now discharged. There will be no sitting of parliament today or even on the morrow. You are all required to return here the day after without fail.'

Sir Richard could hardly believe his ears. Sir Ranulf, aware that something momentous had happened, kept asking him to tell him what was being said, all the while shoving the cow horn in his face.

The Great Hall by now was full of noise and angry mutterings, none of which disconcerted Sir Roger Mortimer. He leaped nimbly from the dais and marched down the aisle. His armed guards followed closely behind him, the noise of their boots echoing round the hall as they marched in step.

'Well, Sir Richard, what has occurred?' Sir Ranulf demanded.

'Something bad,' Richard replied into his horn. 'Something very bad indeed. The Earl of Kent and others have been arrested, and we are all required to attend here again two days hence.'

'Treachery!' Sir Ranulf bellowed.

Richard leaned close to the cow horn as people all around them rose to leave the Great Hall. 'High treason, Sir Ranulf. That is what the Earl of March just said the king's uncle is accused of.'

The old knight opened and closed his mouth in exasperation, then lowered his hearing horn to his side as they too stood to go. 'The Earl of Kent — a traitor! This is treachery and infamy, Sir Richard. I shall hear no more!'

Concerned at the loudness of the old judge's sudden outburst, Richard once again raised a finger to his lips.

Sir Ranulf stared at him for a moment then, raising his voice as loudly as before, he declared, 'A traitor! By Jove, I'll have none of it.'

3

Winchester was awash with gossip the next day. The news that the late King Edward II's younger brother Edmund of Woodstock, the Earl of Kent, had been arrested on a charge of high treason was the subject of conversation in every manor house, town house, tavern and brothel in the city.

The city itself swelled as more armed men of Queen Isabella and her favourite, Sir Roger Mortimer, the Earl of March were stationed at all the places of importance. The city gates were closed without warning, and every farmer, merchant, pilgrim and noble was questioned and their goods and belongings inspected for hidden arms. The city of Winchester had been locked down.

'I could get drunk in any tavern in Winchester without spending anything at all, for as soon as I mention that I am your man I suddenly have friends hanging on my every word and the ale flows freely.'

'But I trust that you say nothing, Hubert,' Richard remarked with a smile. He himself had many discussions with other judges and knights like Sir Ranulf and had garnered their opinions. Knowing how well Hubert could tap into the gossip on the street, he had sent him out with a purse of money to see what he could learn from the market and local hostelries. Hubert had done so with alacrity.

'I could tell them anything, my lord, but since I know nothing I merely wink a lot and let my drinking friends tell me what they think.'

'And what do they think?'

'Why, just about everything, my lord. I have yet to meet a man who does not hold an opinion, although most are wary of being openly critical about the queen or her lover.'

'They call Sir Roger Mortimer her lover?'

'Aye, and usually in more colourful language than that, my lord. Sir Roger is not overly popular here, whereas the Earl of Kent is. By all accounts he is unaccountably good looking and well-liked by the ladies.'

'What do they make of the armed guards that are abroad everywhere? And of the closure of the city gates?'

'There is a feeling that something is about to happen. Some worry that the city is going to be attacked. Others say it is to prevent any disturbance or uprising from within the city.' Hubert took a hefty swig from a mug of milk he had brought to Richard's room with him and then wiped away the tiny white flecks that had splashed onto his moustache and beard with the back of his hand. 'Excuse me, my lord, but I find that milk always calms the stomach after a gallon of ale.'

Richard smiled. 'I wonder at your capacity for ale, but if milk on top of it keeps you well, then drink away.' He had never seen Hubert look remotely drunk.

Hubert supped the rest of his milk, then asked, 'What do you think, my lord?'

Richard had been reading documents and writing on vellum at a table by the window and sat for a moment, stroking the feather tip of the quill against his clean-shaven cheek. 'I am as unsure as anyone, Hubert. Sir Roger Mortimer and his inner circle have not been available today, and no one that I know has been able to find out where the Earl of Kent is being held or how he is being treated. He could be at this moment in a dungeon, or being submitted to torture. It is a mystery, and all we can do is speculate. But that may change tomorrow.'

'How so, my lord?'

'While you have been drinking ale all day, I received this message, which will also have been delivered to all due to attend the parliament tomorrow. I am to watch the proceedings of the trial of the Earl of Kent. It is not signed, but it states it is by order of the king and it bears the seal of the Lord Protector.'

'A trial? So soon?'

'Exactly what I thought, Hubert.'

'But how did they know that you were staying in this hostelry, my lord?'

Richard clicked his tongue. 'A clerk took down the details of where everyone was staying as we arrived at the castle yesterday. I had thought little of it at the time for I am a mere provincial sergeant-at-law and judge, but many of the nobles were angered that they had not been permitted to stay at Winchester Castle upon Sir Roger Mortimer's orders.'

Hubert frowned. 'And with the city gates being closed and all of the armed guards positioned around the city, it is almost as if extra precautions are being taken to ensure His Majesty's safety.'

Richard nodded. 'That, and perhaps also to make sure that there is no disturbance or protestation during this parliament's deliberations.'

'But surely that is not something that would normally be anticipated, my lord?'

'It isn't, Hubert. Which makes me think that there may have been another reason for so many judges being summoned to attend. And that then begs the question, was it known that the arrest and subsequent trial of the Earl of Kent had been planned well ahead?'

The atmosphere in the Great Hall the next day was quite unlike anything Richard had experienced before. All the nobility, knights, sheriffs and judges had taken their places as they had done two days before. Sir Ranulf was already seated when Richard took his place beside him. The Lincoln judge was waiting with his cow horn ready in his hand.

'I don't like this, Sir Richard. I don't like it at all. How can the old king's brother — the new king's uncle — be tried in parliament?'

Richard spoke into the cow horn. 'A question that every sergeant-at-law here will have been pondering, Sir Ranulf. It is without precedent in English law.'

More people filed in and sat. Snatches of conversation all around him proved Richard right. All the lawyers were equally astonished that a trial was to be held and confused about how it should be conducted.

A trumpet sounded and everyone stood up. The doors to the entrance opened and heavily armed guards marched in and made their way along the aisle, before spacing out and then standing at attention. Immediately, a royal procession entered, headed by the youthful King Edward III walking a step ahead of Sir Roger Mortimer. Behind him walked a thin man in an ill-fitting coif and black lawyer's robes. He was carrying a sheaf of documents.

'Is that old Robert Howel?' Sir Ranulf said, his voice still undesirably loud even though he thought it a whisper.

Richard signalled for him to lower his voice and then whispered into the cow horn. 'Yes, the coroner to the royal household. It looks as if he is going to preside.'

King Edward mounted the dais and sat on his throne beneath the great Round Table. Sir Roger mounted the steps and stood to the right of him. Robert Howel the coroner took his place at a high desk that had been brought in and positioned below the dais.

At a nod of assent from the king, Sir Roger boomed out the command to sit. Then, after a bow to the sovereign, he began to speak. 'My liege, it grieves me beyond measure, but today I must crave your indulgence and bring to trial a heinous traitor to you and to the realm.'

'So I understand, my lord,' King Edward said, his voice filled with emotion. 'Name this traitor.'

'It is your father's younger brother, Edmund of Woodstock.'

Without further ado, Mortimer signalled to a captain of the guard and called out in a loud voice, 'Bring in the prisoner!'

There were gasps as Edmund of Woodstock, the Earl of Kent was brought in, led by a chain looped between his shackled wrists. He was wearing a dirt-stained tunic and he looked bedraggled. His blond hair was lank and he had a bruise upon one cheek and a healing cut on his lower lip.

There was a collective gasp of horror and alarm at the sight of him, for this was the king's own uncle.

'Edward, I beseech —' Sir Edmund began.

'Prisoner, be silent!' Sir Roger cried. 'Bring him forth to stand before His Majesty.'

Richard cast a glance at the king. Even from a distance, he could tell that he was not comfortable.

'Sire, these proceedings will be presided over by Robert Howel, your coroner.'

King Edward nodded at the official standing behind his high desk and Howel bowed.

'I shall prosecute this case on your behalf, Sire,' said Mortimer.

The Earl of Kent cleared his throat and with a quaking voice called out, 'Edward, my liege, I know nothing of these matters that I am accused of, but —'

'Silence!' Mortimer boomed out. 'The court has not yet heard the claims against the accused.'

Turning to the assembly, he pulled out a rolled document from beneath his belt, unfurled it and started to read.

'Sir Edmund, Earl of Kent, you should understand that it behoves us to say that you are a deadly enemy and traitor to our liege lord, King Edward of England — whom we ask Almighty God to save and keep — and also a common enemy unto the realm.'

He raised his eyes and glared at the noble standing before him in chains, as if relishing his discomfort.

'You have these many days been secretively and by devious means planning the deliverance of your brother Sir Edward, sometime King of England, who was deposed from his royalty by common assent of all the lords of England —'

Again he stopped and quite deliberately looked around the hall, his gaze momentarily falling on certain lords who had been present and involved in the deposition of King Edward II.

Richard noted the reactions of these nobles, who included Adam Orleton, the Bishop of Worcester, John Stratford, the Bishop of Winchester, Sir William Trussell and Sir Thomas Blunt.

He also saw that Sir William de Montagu, Sir William de Bohun, Sir William Clinton and Sir John Neville, the king's friends, were standing together and all looked concerned. The king was studiously avoiding looking at any of them.

Mortimer glanced down at the document and continued reading. 'And in impairing thus, you sought to undermine our lord the king's estate, and also the rule of this realm.'

There was silence in the Great Hall as everyone took in the enormity of the charge. Then there were mumblings.

'Is he saying the old king is still alive, Richard?' Sir Ranulf asked, managing to keep his voice low for once.

'Indeed, that is the charge,' Richard replied into the cow horn. 'Let us hear what evidence there is.'

Edmund of Woodstock gasped in horror. 'This is a lie! My lord, King Edward, my nephew, surely you do not —?'

'Silence, or you will be silenced with a gag and a muzzle, sirrah!' Mortimer called out. 'All you are required to do is acknowledge that you understand the charges.' He waited a few seconds, then asked impatiently, 'Well, do you?'

Edmund of Woodstock held himself upright and nodded. 'I understand them and refute them most strongly. Edward, please, discharge this nonsensical charge.'

The king sat uneasily, his as-yet beardless cheeks growing red. 'The charges are grave,' he returned loudly. 'I would hear the evidence against the prisoner.'

'Prisoner?' Sir Edmund repeated, numbly. 'I am of royal blood, my liege. I am your uncle, as is my brother Thomas, Earl of Norfolk.'

Casting an eye around those at the front of the hall, Richard spotted the Earl of Norfolk, who bore a resemblance to both Edward II, the former king, and to Edmund of Woodstock. The noble had tears upon his cheeks and was shaking his head in disbelief.

'This trial shall now hear how in the prisoner's own words — ' Mortimer began.

'No! I am of royal blood, and I am a peer of the realm. If I am to be tried, then I demand that it be before my peers.'

Mortimer shook his head. 'The charge is of high treason. It is too heinous a charge to be tried by the few. You must be tried before this parliament and before your king. And that is now!'

He snapped his fingers in Robert Howel's direction and held out his hand with the document from which he had read the charges. Immediately, the coroner approached the dais with a letter. He handed it to the Lord Protector and took the other back to his sheaf of papers on the high desk.

Mortimer held up the letter and pointed to a seal. 'This is a letter that the prisoner, Sir Edmund of Woodstock, sent to a royal castle with the instructions that it be given to his brother, the late King Edward the Second. It was given to a knight who is loyal to our king. Look at this, Edmund of Woodstock. Is it your seal?'

'I … I cannot see so far.'

'Then I will show you it close, sirrah!' Mortimer strode over to the Earl of Kent and showed him. 'Well, is it your seal?'

The earl nodded. 'It is my seal, but it is of no great consequence. I send many letters.' Again, he addressed his nephew upon the throne. 'Edward, I meant nothing more than —'

Mortimer opened the letter and held it high for the assembly to see. 'It is written in a neat hand. Do you recognise the hand that wrote this, Edmund of Woodstock? Because I most certainly do.'

The earl swallowed hard. 'It is in the hand of my wife, Margaret Wake, Countess of Kent.'

'Who is my cousin,' Mortimer stated for all to hear. 'Yet is it your signature?'

'It … it is.'

'And your seal?'

'Yes,' the Earl of Kent replied hoarsely.

'So, it was written upon your dictation?'

'I … I do not recollect this letter. As I said, I send so many.'

'Then allow me to refresh your memory.'

Returning to the dais, Mortimer read the letter out in a loud voice.

'Worships and reverence, with a brother's legeance and subjection. Sir Knight, worshipful and dear brother, if you please, I pray heartily that you are of good comfort, for I shall ordain for you that soon you shall come out of prison, and be delivered of that disease in which you find yourself. Your lordship should know that I have the assent of almost all the great lords of England, with all their apparel, that is to say, with armour and willingness to bear arms, and with treasure without limit, in order to maintain and help your quarrel as you shall be king again as you were before, and that they all, prelates, earls, dukes and barons, have sworn to me upon a Bible.'

There had been silence throughout the reading, but now there were exclamations of astonishment. Richard was unable to discern people's true reaction, for all present were aware of how perilous it was to express any view. But several questions immediately sprang to his legal mind as a sergeant-at-law.

First, did this plot to free the former king — for whom a royal funeral had been held in Gloucester Abbey — indicate that he was actually still alive and being kept prisoner somewhere?

Second, who would have anything to gain by keeping him prisoner and keeping it secret?

And third, who were the prelates and nobles involved in such a plot?

Again Richard looked around, this time studying those nobles present for any sign of fear of exposure.

Mortimer continued, addressing Edmund of Woodstock. 'Do you admit that you dictated this letter to my cousin, Margaret Wake, who was married to Lord John Comyn, who died at the Battle of Bannockburn before she married you?'

The Earl of Kent bent his head and muttered assent.

Mortimer turned to the king. 'You can see why I say this is high treason, Your Majesty?'

King Edward leaned forward and pointed a finger at his uncle. 'Why have you brought this upon yourself? You attended my father's funeral. You saw his coffin. You even tried to comfort me upon my loss — both you and the Earl of Norfolk, your brother and my other uncle.'

Under the king's accusing eyes the Earl of Kent visibly trembled. He blustered and started to weep.

'He was my ... my brother, my liege. I only wanted him back ... not as king, but as he was — Edward of Caernarfon.'

'That is a lie!' cried Mortimer, holding the letter in the air. 'You are condemned by your own words.' He held the letter in his left hand and ran a finger down the lines. 'You said: ...*all the great lords of England, with all their apparel, that is to say, with armour and willingness to bear arms, and with treasure without limit, in order to maintain and help your quarrel as you shall be king again as you were before.*'

Woodstock quaked. 'I did not mean —'

'You clearly say that your aim was to put your brother back on the throne and that you had many lords swear on the Bible that they would bear arms to achieve this. You intended rebellion against our King Edward the Third and that Edward the Second, whom the lords had deposed in favour of our king, would be put on the throne again.'

'No, I only meant —'

'There is no other meaning, sirrah. Now tell us, here and now, who are these lords and prelates?'

For the next half an hour, Mortimer interrogated the Earl of Kent. At first the prisoner tried to answer firmly, but then his answers grew increasingly garbled and confused.

Richard watched and could not help but feel increasingly sympathetic towards the earl. He was well aware that most people would crumble under a fierce onslaught from an interrogator. And Mortimer had the full power of his position as Lord Protector. It was also clear that the king was not going to intercede on his behalf.

Yet for all this, the earl did not name anyone.

'We shall have names,' Mortimer said at last. 'The traitors shall be hunted down and arrested, and they will face the king's law. This may include those that failed to obey the summons to attend his parliament. None are so great and mighty that they can escape justice.'

Richard immediately assumed that he meant Sir Henry, Earl of Lancaster. He was one of the most powerful lords of the land, being a first cousin to the late King Edward II, and brother to Thomas, who had been executed at Pontefract and who had become known as Saint Thomas after miracles started to occur at his tomb in Pontefract Priory.

It was well known that Henry of Lancaster had no love for Sir Roger Mortimer. Richard had heard that he was not well, but also assumed that he had stayed away because he feared for his safety.

Perhaps Edmund of Woodstock should have been equally circumspect, he thought.

King Edward signalled for Mortimer to come to him, and after a few moments of whispered conversation Mortimer gestured for Robert Howel to come to the foot of the dais, where the king and Mortimer gave him instructions.

The coroner bowed, returned to his high desk and started writing. When he had finished, he poured dusting powder made of crushed shells over the parchment to dry the ink and then blew it away, before he again walked to the foot of the dais and showed the parchment to Mortimer. In turn, the Earl of March showed it to the king, who read it and passed it back to Mortimer.

Taking the parchment back, the coroner made some amendments, presumed by all to be on the instructions of the king and Sir Roger Mortimer.

'The coroner Robert Howel shall now read the judgement of this court,' Mortimer announced.

Richard could scarcely believe that a judgement was to be passed without any adequate legal representation having been made on behalf of the accused. He listened as the coroner read aloud from the parchment.

'Sir Edmund, you have admitted in this court, before your peers and before parliament and all the judges of the land, that this is your letter, dictated by yourself. The tenor of this is that you planned and were on the verge of putting this plan into action, to deliver the body of that worshipful knight, Sir Edward, sometime King of England, who was your brother. You wanted to help him become king again, so that he could govern his people as he did beforehand, thus deposing the state of your liege lord — the present king whom God had chosen and who was anointed in his name.

'It is therefore the will of this court that you shall lose both life and limb, and that your heirs shall be disinherited forevermore, save the grace of our lord the king.'

The earl shrieked and looked about to collapse, but then regained himself. He held his shackled wrists up and pleaded with the king.

'My liege king, nephew, we share the same royal blood. Have mercy upon me.'

'Take the prisoner away!' Mortimer cried. 'His Majesty has to deliberate on when the execution shall take place.'

The assembly looked on in stunned silence as the Earl of Kent was led away, still loudly protesting his innocence.

After whispering to the king, Mortimer made another announcement. 'The king will return tomorrow and this parliament and court within it shall reconvene. You must all attend when the condemned prisoner will hear His Majesty's decision.'

4

News that the Earl of Kent had been put on trial and was to be executed for high treason had spread across the city by word of mouth. Inevitably, the words became distorted so that multiple independent rumours abounded.

Some thought that he had been summarily executed. Others heard that he and Mortimer had come to blows in parliament and that Kent had been cast into a dungeon. Yet others heard that the king had ordered that he be submitted to the rack.

'My lord, the marketplace is rife with tales and there is fear that there will be rebellion and war,' Hubert told his master.

Richard had attended mass at the cathedral while Hubert had gone information-gathering after they had broken their fast at the tavern. He was writing at the table by the mullioned window when Hubert returned, well wrapped against the cold in his travelling cloak. He had composed a letter to his wife, the Lady Wilhelmina, to explain that his visit to attend the parliament had been complicated by a legal case that was being tried as a matter of urgency. As a result, he and Hubert would be delayed a few days more, but he would explain all upon his return. He had already written a similar letter to his father-in-law, Sir Thomas Deyville, the Steward of Sandal Castle. He had been careful not to say more in either letter, lest it be intercepted. Wilhelmina would understand that something dire was occurring. Her bluff old father was less erudite and would merely grumble that the affairs of the Manor Court were being neglected.

'I have written to Lady Wilhelmina, and I have asked her to let your wife know that we are delayed,' Richard told Hubert as he lay down his quill. He picked up a goblet and sipped the watered-down wine. 'As to the fears of the good folk of Winchester, they may well be right, Hubert. Who knows what may happen if Sir Roger Mortimer follows through with this execution?'

'Sir Roger, you say, my lord? Not King Edward?'

'The whole affair smacks of devilish cunning, Hubert. I fear that the king has been placed in an untenable position. Edward may sit upon the throne, but it is Mortimer and Queen Isabella who rule the land. It is they who will decide what happens next. They govern the land as if they were playing chess. And in this instance the Earl of Kent has been relegated from a royal piece to that of a pawn.'

Hubert looked momentarily puzzled. 'Chess is a game that I have yet to learn, my lord, but I think I understand. They are using the earl as if he is an ordinary man, a soldier, and not the king's uncle.'

'Indeed, and the question as to whether King Edward the Second is alive or not is at the centre of this horrific situation. If he is dead, then why would the Earl of Kent and these other nobles and prelates plan to rescue him from the place they thought he was held prisoner? Unless that was a mere ploy and they were actually planning to attack and take a royal castle. That in itself is an act of treason.'

'But if it is true and the old king is still alive?'

'Then they could depose King Edward the Third. So you see how the king is in an impossible position. He could not admit that he knew the king was alive all this time; if he is alive, then young Edward would be at risk of being deposed by his own father and uncle. And if he was deposed, the argument could be made that he had committed treason against the anointed King of England.'

Hubert puffed out his cheeks. 'This is a situation that grows more dangerous for the Earl of Kent with every passing hour.' He thought for a moment. 'But the Earl of Kent is not the only uncle to the king, is he, my lord? The Earl of Norfolk is his younger brother. Is he involved?'

'That I do not know. He was there when his brother was being charged with these crimes, but he said nothing. Perhaps we will find out this day if there is further news disclosed at the parliament meeting.'

The Grand Hall seemed a particularly cold and forbidding place that morning. The king's entry was delayed, which caused an increase in the number of muttered conversations as the assembly waited and speculated. As before, the hubbub in the hall was silenced by the entry of the guards, and then of King Edward, Sir Roger Mortimer and Robert Howel.

'Bring in the prisoner!' barked Mortimer, once more having taken a stance to the right of the seated monarch.

Richard stared aghast at the Earl of Kent. The bruise on his cheek had turned purple and the cut on his lip had scabbed over. Yet it was his expression of abject fear and misery that was most apparent.

Mortimer motioned for the coroner to step forward. 'It is His Majesty's wish that you all hear a confession made by the condemned prisoner since he last stood here before you all.'

Robert Howel held out a parchment and began to read. 'Let it be known that on this date, March the sixteenth, in the year of our lord 1330, the prisoner, Sir Edmund, the Earl of Kent, solemnly acknowledges that the Pope, John the Twenty-second of that name charged him to bring about the release of his brother, Edward of Caernarfon, the former King of England.

Further, that the Holy Father did promise to finance this most unholy venture.'

There was disbelief on most people's faces, but the king stared ahead in stony silence, as if he were a statue.

The coroner then told them that Kent had admitted that many lords and clerics were involved in this plot, including the Archbishop of York, William Melton, who had pledged five thousand pounds towards the plot. He had also named the Bishop of Durham, Lewis de Beaumont, Sir William de la Zouche, the Keeper of the King's Wardrobe, Sir Ingelram de Berengar, Sir Hugh FitzWarin, the Earl of Mar, Lady Isabella de Vesci and several others.

Richard frowned on hearing the names, especially those of William Melton, Bishop Lewis de Beaumont and the Lady Vesci. He knew all three personally, and had actually saved the Archbishop of York's life some years previously.

He was still thinking about it when Robert Howel continued to read out the earl's confession, detailing the involvement of several friars.

'...*yet among these friars one in particular was skilled in the occult arts and told me in London that he had conjured up a demon in a black mass. He told me that this demon had revealed to him in a vision that my brother, he who was King Edward the Second until his deposition, was being held at Corfe Castle. I had doubted him at first, until I witnessed with my own eyes him having a fit such as he was plagued with ever since he had studied the art of conjuration. He told me that demons sought to enter our world through him and he had ever to be prepared to do battle with them and subdue them in such fits. Yet each time, these demons would try to tempt him by giving him glimpses of things that are kept secret and of things that have not yet happened...*'

Richard felt Sir Ranulf nudge his arm. He was sitting beside him as usual, with his cow horn at his ear. It was pointed directly at the coroner.

He silently mouthed: *Did he just say that a priest called up a demon?*

Richard nodded.

At a black mass?

When Richard again nodded, the deaf knight shook his head in disbelief and made the sign of the cross over his heart.

As the coroner concluded his reading of the confession, Mortimer addressed the Earl of Kent. 'Well, sirrah, is that a true confession?'

The Earl of Kent nodded and turning to King Edward, held up his manacled wrists. 'My liege lord, my dearest nephew, I … I meant no harm to you. My only desire was to rescue my brother. I beseech you, have mercy upon me. I am a wretched miscreant of a man and I will submit to any punishment you choose, but please, do not take my life. I have four children.'

He stared at his nephew, whose face was pale yet impassive.

Richard saw that the young king's jaw was clenched and that he held the arms of his throne tightly, as if determined not to show any emotion.

The earl continued to plead. 'Edward … I —'

'Do not dare to address His Majesty in familiar terms!' Sir Roger Mortimer roared.

The Earl of Kent bowed his head. 'My abject apologies, Your Majesty … please, I will do anything. Why, I will walk through the streets of Winchester with nothing but this shirt … with a rope about my neck…'

Still the king was unmoved.

'…or to London, even. I will walk it barefoot.'

'Enough!' cried Mortimer. 'We have heard this despicable confession from the condemned man. His Majesty has already decreed that the execution of this traitor shall take place outside the castle walls in three days' time. Take him out of His Majesty's sight. God save the king.'

Sobbing loudly, the earl continued to beg for mercy as he was manhandled out of the Great Hall.

Only then did King Edward move. He nodded to Mortimer then stood. The royal guards rapped their pikestaffs on the floor and stood ready to escort the king from the hall. Everyone immediately stood and bowed as without a word King Edward left rapidly.

Once the great doors had been closed, Mortimer moved to the queen's empty throne and sat down. He stared stonily at the assembly, almost challenging anyone to talk.

He's going to dismiss us now, Richard thought.

Instead, Sir Roger brushed his hands together as if to remove something on his palms. Then, examining his fingernails and without standing, he addressed them.

'His Majesty the King has instructed me to inform you that he expects you all to attend the execution at ten o'clock in the morning three days hence. And once that is out of the way, this parliament assembly will reconvene at two o'clock on that afternoon. We have important business of parliament to discuss, particularly concerning some grants that we need to make.

'His Majesty also appreciates that this must have been a difficult time for everyone here present, so that is why he is suspending the assembly until after the execution of the traitorous Earl of Kent. Until we meet again you should all reflect upon what has occurred this day and what is about to happen. Those reflections, however, should be solely one's own and not those of any groups from this assembly.'

There was no noise in the hall whatsoever. No one was in any doubt as to what Mortimer meant. There should be no discussion, no question of any protest or of any action.

It was a cold, drizzly day when Edmund of Woodstock, the Earl of Kent, was led out in chains before a huge crowd that had gathered in front of the castle wall. Sir Roger Mortimer stood upon the stage that had been erected and on which the block and the executioner's axe awaited.

The earl was brought before the crowd and made to mount the steps.

'Where is the executioner?' Mortimer demanded.

A captain of the guards diffidently replied, 'He refuses to execute one of royal blood, Sir Roger.'

Mortimer furiously ordered one of the men-at-arms to do the deed, but one after the other they all refused.

Richard and Hubert were amidst the increasingly restless crowd, whose attendance in the cold rain was obligatory.

'Is King Edward not watching, my lord?' Hubert asked Richard.

'He may be from one of the turrets, but I cannot see him. Nor Queen Isabella, who is not only the Earl of Kent's sister-in-law as she was married to King Edward the Second, but also his cousin.'

The bells struck the hours until finally a man called Gideon of Twyford, a dung farmer and public latrine cleaner, was brought out. He had been due to be hanged that day, but because of Edmund of Woodstock's execution being arranged so hastily he had been granted a day's reprieve. Having failed to find a single guard or soldier willing to wield the axe,

Mortimer told his clerk to offer any of the prisoners in the Winchester jail a pardon if they were willing to do the deed.

'I will, most willingly,' Gideon of Twyford had replied. 'I was a butcher before ill luck brought me to clearing the dung that everyone makes.'

'What was this man's crime?' Mortimer asked when Gideon of Twyford was brought before him.

'He killed a man with his bare hands in a drunken rage,' the clerk reported.

'Why were you in a rage, Gideon of Twyford?' Mortimer asked.

'A surly fellow picked a fight with me, my lord. While I was drinking and playing hazard.'

'About what?'

'He claimed I had seduced his wife.'

'Had you?'

The latrine cleaner shrugged his shoulders. 'I had been drinking a lot, my lord. I may have done. I didn't look too closely at the wench.'

Mortimer frowned. 'Will you cut off the prisoner's head, even knowing who he is?'

'If I am pardoned, I don't care whose head you want hacking off. I'll do it.'

So, at last, a shivering Edmund of Woodstock was blindfolded and guided to the block. A priest intoned some Latin and was relieved to leave the platform. And then, after taking a couple of practice swings with the heavy axe, Gideon of Twyford hewed off the Earl of Kent's head.

The crowd cried out in disgust and many retched and vomited.

'Pick it up, as I told you,' Sir Roger Mortimer ordered Gideon as blood continued to pump out of the headless corpse slumped over the block, held there by the shackles on the wrists.

Laying the axe aside and grasping the head by its now blood-stained blond hair, the latrine cleaner held it aloft as he called out, 'Behold the head of a traitor!'

That was normally the sign for people to cheer or call out, 'God Save the King!' But there was nothing but silence.

5

Richard had been astonished by the sanguine manner in which Sir Roger Mortimer had carried on with the affairs of parliament when the assembly reconvened at two o'clock in the afternoon. It was as if the public execution of the Earl of Kent were of little consequence.

Mortimer made a case for the raising of taxes on the clergy and upon the common people for the defence of Gascony, which was given assent without any debate. Even more surprising, they discovered that the grants he had mentioned were in fact titles, estates and honours for himself, his sons and those nobles in his and Queen Isabella's inner circle.

In the king's absence Mortimer formally closed the session, but not before he read out a list of forty arrest warrants that were to be issued. These were the names mentioned in the Earl of Kent's confession that had been read out by Robert Howel, the coroner. To Richard's horror, this included the earl's wife and their four children.

'And according to the law,' Mortimer went on, 'the traitorous Earl of Kent's lands in Leicestershire, Gloucestershire, Surrey, Lincolnshire, Derbyshire, Wiltshire, Nottinghamshire and Rutland are all forfeited and their future custodianship will be decided by His Majesty in due course.'

As Richard and the rest of the assembly filtered out of the Great Hall he was accosted by a court clerk, who was delivering sealed messages to some, but not all, of those who had attended. Outside the castle he broke open the seal and read the message. It was an invitation from King Edward and the royal family, which was in actuality a summons, to a feast to be held in the Great East Hall of Wolvesey Castle, the official residence of His Grace, John Stratford, the Bishop of Winchester.

No sooner had Richard returned to his hostelry than he received another message, this time from Sir Ranulf Fermont. He had sent his servant to ask Richard to meet him at the Church of St Swithun, just above the Kingsgate, one of the entrances to the city. Richard had previously been struck by the unusual building, for it actually formed part of the city wall. Sir Ranulf had told him that he was staying close by in one of the taverns.

'Thank you for coming here, Sir Richard,' the old knight said as Richard joined him at a pew in the back of the church. 'I like this place, for although it is part of the city wall, I think it is one of the few places where there are unlikely to be ears listening to what we say.' He gave one of his rare grins. 'And when you have the hearing impediment that I have, that is important since as you well know, I talk loudly and ask folk to speak loudly into my horn.'

Judging by the way that everyone at the assembly had dispersed, Richard was sure that few of his fellow judges and knights wished to be seen conversing in groups. However, like Sir Ranulf, he was eager to know what others thought of the execution and the successive meeting.

'I think that your senses are not all so diminished as your hearing, Ranulf,' Richard said with a knowing smile. 'Your eyesight is as keen as that of a young kestrel.'

Sir Ranulf looked around and then laughed. 'You are right there, Richard. I think the good Lord sometimes does that. He gives and he takes, so when one sense is much reduced he enhances another. I am fortunate to still have some hearing, thanks to my trumpet here, but I see well enough and my nose is almost as good as that of my hounds in Lincoln.'

He sniffed loudly as if to demonstrate, then wrinkled his nose as if detecting an unpleasant odour. 'And by all that is holy, we have witnessed a sight that I never would have thought possible until I came to Winchester.'

'Agreed, Ranulf. And yet we judges have been told by the Earl of March that we must uphold the laws that parliament agreed to.'

'We agreed to what?'

Richard realised that he had dropped his voice below the level he usually used to talk to the old judge. He repeated himself in a louder voice, adding, 'That was what I at first assumed was the reason we judges and lawyers were told to attend the parliament, after we had been summoned to pledge our allegiance to His Majesty King Edward the Third. The horrors that we have witnessed these last few days make me think otherwise.'

Sir Ranulf tapped the side of his nose and gave a loud chuckle. 'Your sense of smell is well developed, too, is it not, Richard? I think you smelled the same stench that I did.'

Richard smiled. He knew that the old knight was a shrewd judge. 'Yes, we were brought here in advance of a plan that was well laid out, rather like a spider's web. The Earl of Kent fell into it with no hope of escape and we were the unwitting witnesses. We were judges of the realm watching a trial that was no trial, but we were powerless to do anything about it. And now we are being sent back to our manors and courts to dispense the laws agreed upon here, though I saw no debate — I merely heard what the Earl of March told us had been decided.'

Sir Ranulf waved his horn. 'Blast this impediment of mine, but I think I caught all that you said. I think we are agreed that we have seen great injustice done to one of royal blood and to his family, and to any who support him. That is why I wanted to talk to you in private about what you thought of the Earl of Kent's confession.'

'I thought it decidedly strange.'

'It smelled of brimstone, Richard,' Sir Ranulf said, nodding his head vigorously. 'It is hard to believe that a demon was conjured up in a black mass by some friar versed in the dark arts. And yet that is what the earl admitted he had said. Can it be true?'

Richard shrugged resignedly. 'I am not well read in these matters, but the clerics present did not seem to raise objections.'

'No one raised objections out of fear, Richard. None dares oppose Sir Roger Mortimer openly, in my opinion. That includes you and I both.'

'We must do whatever is best for the country and King Edward's realm,' Richard replied. 'Yet it worries me that we were given no more information other than a friar had conjured a demon. Who that was, where they are from and who they are accountable to are all questions we ought to seek answers to, yet it was all just accepted as fact and the whole thing moved on so quickly.'

Sir Ranulf had his horn directed at Richard. He nodded. 'In my court I dislike unanswered questions, Richard. And I worry for the safety of the Earl of Kent's family.' He sighed. 'I saw that you also received a sealed message from a clerk. Are you going to this feast at Bishop Stratford's palace?'

'I fear there is no choice in the matter.'

Sir Ranulf frowned. 'I scarcely feel like feasting after the atrocity today, yet I suppose we will have to at least force some food and wine down our throats. Did you know that Sir Roger Mortimer set a precedent by holding a feast like this to celebrate after they executed the younger Hugh le Despenser?'

Richard nodded. 'Yes, I had heard that, although both Hugh and his father were generally very unpopular, whereas the Earl of Kent was the brother of one king and the uncle of another. And he was popular with the people.'

'Aye, this is an altogether different affair. Not quite what we lawyers would consider a legal principle, *stare decisis*, but it bodes ill for all if this is adopted as a custom, *mos pro lege*.'

Richard smiled as once again Sir Ranulf demonstrated his firm grasp of English law.

'Time will tell how the populace will react to the news,' he said. 'Whatever the Earl of March and Queen Isabella think.'

'Well, speaking for myself, I worry that food will taste foul for many days from now, and the few morsels I take at this feast may even stick in my gullet.'

Richard clicked his tongue. 'Again, I agree, but at least then mayhap we can return to our homes,' he returned.

Sir Ranulf nodded. 'Not before time. Are you travelling by way of London?'

'Yes, and then by the Great North Road to Pontefract, then to Wakefield.'

'Perhaps we could travel together, Richard. Safety in numbers, so to say.'

Richard smiled. 'If there be such a thing as safety in England these days. Yes, it would be a good idea, Ranulf.'

'Then let us hope we hear and see no more of devilry and plotting at this feast.'

'I have no great appetite, Hubert,' Richard said as his man helped him dress for the feast.

'I could go in your stead, if I shaved off my beard, my lord,' Hubert jested. 'I was also appalled at having to witness the earl's execution, but my stomach still craves to be filled on a regular basis. I can almost imagine all the roast…'

'Enough, Hubert. I fear that it would take more than shaving your beard for you to go in my place to Wolvesey Castle without being challenged. I am well known, but the security around the king and his family will be tightened up beyond measure at present. And as we already know, Sir Roger Mortimer and Queen Isabella are always especially careful.'

Richard put on the blue hose that Hubert handed him, then a blue tunic and a darker blue half-cape, before pulling on a pair of calf leather boots.

He tossed a purse to Hubert. 'I would not wish you to go hungry, my friend. Go and eat and drink. And while you are doing that, do a little more delving.'

Hubert grinned. 'Delving, my lord?'

'Find out what you can about the Earl of Kent's executioner.'

'May I ask why, my lord?'

'I'd like to know what sort of a man he is. How did he feel about smiting off the head of the king's uncle?'

'We heard that he was a condemned criminal, my lord.'

'I know, but did he relish his task, or does he feel any guilt? Any remorse?'

'I will try to track him down, my lord.'

'There is something else to ask if you do find him.'

'My lord?'

'The last person to speak to someone facing death on the block is the executioner. It would be interesting to know if the earl said anything that only he heard.'

People were already entering the Great East Hall of Wolvesey Castle, Bishop Stratford's palace. Richard was somewhat relieved that they were not being entertained at Winchester Castle, where so much drama had been played out over the past several days. Nonetheless, entering the palace was a daunting experience, for armed guards were posted at the entrance and also at various positions inside the hall. Huge fireplaces had been lit, and it was obvious the hall had been arranged for a festive occasion.

By the time Richard reached his place, as he had been directed by a clerk at the entrance, the hall was already full of people. They stood behind wooden chairs on either side of two rows of linen-covered tables arranged along the length of the room. Unlike at the parliament assembly, there were ladies present, the wives of those lords and knights who either lived near to Winchester or who had travelled with their husbands.

Yet it was a noticeably smaller affair. It was obvious that many of those who had attended the assembly had not been invited. This made Richard wonder again why those present this evening had been singled out.

Like the Great Hall at Winchester Castle, there was a dais at one end, and it had been specially arranged for royalty. The thrones had been brought to the palace and placed behind a large table that had been prepared for the royal party.

A group of musicians occupied an ornately decorated minstrels' gallery high on a wall to the right of the dais, filling the air with the sounds of the harp, vielle, shawm and lute.

Two of the minstrels sang, their voices complementing the music beautifully.

Looking around the hall, Richard was pleased to see that Sir Ranulf was standing a few seats down from him on the other side of the table. They acknowledged each other with a nod and then engaged in conversation with their neighbours. Sir Ranulf kept his cow horn next to one ear, moving his head towards whoever was talking.

Richard had been placed between Sir John Maltravers and his wife Millicent de Berkeley. He was a hard-faced man with a red moustache and a lazy left eye, while she was a good-looking woman in her mid-twenties. Smiling at her, Richard saw quite clearly the resemblance to her brother, Baron Thomas de Berkeley, who was sitting next to Sir Ranulf, while his wife, Lady Margaret Mortimer, bore a striking resemblance to her father, Sir Roger Mortimer.

Is this a mere coincidence, Richard mused, *or is it a deliberate contrivance? There are about a quarter of the number that attended the assembly, but why have we all been selected? What makes us special?*

Glancing surreptitiously around, he noted several faces who had been staunch supporters of the late King Edward II, or who had either performed well under him or had done him service. Like Ranulf and himself, they had been placed between husband and wife, or between two knights or lords who were firmly associated with Sir Roger Mortimer.

And similarly, those knights whom he knew to be close friends or advisors to King Edward III were also buttressed between Mortimer adherents. He saw Sir William de Montagu, William Clinton and John Neville, but though he looked around the hall he could not see young Sir William de Bohun.

This is no chance matter, Richard now thought. *Sir Roger Mortimer wishes to see whether we are sympathetic to him and Queen*

Isabella or not. If not, our positions and mayhap even our lives could be at risk if we be perceived as a threat. I must be exceedingly careful, as must we all.

He noticed some servants removing three of the seats and wondered if they had been allocated to nobles such as Sir William de Bohun.

The fact that Sir John Maltravers and his brother-in-law Thomas de Berkeley were closely associated with Mortimer through marriage made the matter even more pointed, for after King Edward II's arrest and imprisonment at Kenilworth Castle under the care of Henry, Earl of Lancaster, the two nobles standing beside Ranulf and himself had been appointed keepers of the king at Berkeley Castle until his unexpected death in 1327. Both had remained in charge of his body until his burial at Gloucester Abbey in December of that year.

The guests continued to stand and converse until the sound of two heavy pikestaffs being thumped upon the stone floor averted everyone's attention to the door. The musicians in the gallery ceased playing as two trumpeters blew a familiar fanfare before a chamberlain announced in a loud voice, 'His Majesty King Edward and Her Majesty Queen Philippa and the royal party.'

All eyes turned to the party as it advanced up the hall between the two long tables, every man bowing as they passed and every lady curtsying.

The king and queen processed hand in hand, followed by Queen Isabella, holding hands with Sir Roger Mortimer. A few paces behind them came the upright figure of Bishop John Stratford.

So, Sir Roger Mortimer is now firmly included as a member of the royal party, Richard mused.

The party mounted the dais and took their seats: two central thrones for the royal couple and two smaller thrones to right and left of them for the queen mother and her lover, the Earl of March. Bishop Stratford sat to the right of Sir Roger Mortimer, thought his chair was placed at a slight distance from the earl, as if to emphasise that he was not part of the royal party.

Mortimer exuded power and arrogance. Queen Isabella was beautiful and, as Richard was all too aware, totally ruthless. Sitting between them King Edward looked uncomfortable, yet the firmness about his jaw showed an innate determination. One could not fail to notice how tightly he held his queen's hand. Queen Philippa smiled a lot and it was clear that her husband drew strength from her.

They are in the same position as Sir Ranulf and I, Richard thought as he took his seat along with the other guests. *We all seem to be entangled in an invisible web, one spun by Sir Roger Mortimer. Or is it by his lover, Queen Isabella?*

6

Hubert had familiarised himself with the city over the past few days while Sir Richard had been occupied. He had already sampled the mead and ale at several taverns and had found it relatively simple to pick up the trail of the Earl of Kent's executioner, for the whole distasteful affair was the talk of Winchester. As he had anticipated, he was directed to the northern quarter, where the lowliest hostelries and brothels were to be found. He had worn his nondescript traveller's cloak, which he made look suitably travel-worn by dragging it in the dirt, taking care to ensure that it was only dirt that he picked up on it before he swung it around his shoulders. Then, armed with a stout walking staff, he began his journey.

He had visited but four establishments — in each of which he had downed a tankard of ale — when he found his quarry.

'I must be the luckiest man in the whole of England,' Gideon of Twyford announced to the drinkers in the Holly Bush Tavern, one of the many hostelries that he liked to frequent near the city gates. The sun had gone down and cheap tallow candles had been lit to illuminate the dark room, which was smoky from the fumes that spilled out from the fireplace.

His voice was loud and slurred from all the ale he had consumed. After cutting off the Earl of Kent's head he had been given a purse with more money to spend than he had ever possessed at one time, including all the purses he had removed from those unwary fellows whose heads he had cracked in one or other of the dark alleys of the city.

He had no shortage of willing listeners, for everyone knew of his part in the death of Sir Edmund. Revelling in his notoriety he cast money like water, buying ale for those keen to listen to him. There were many with a great thirst that needed quenching.

'There I was, waiting to have my neck stretched, when that traitor to the king saved me.' He hawked noisily and spat on the reed-covered floor. 'Sir Roger Mortimer, God bless him, pardoned me and gave me a purse of coins for my trouble.'

'Was it messy, Gideon?' asked one of the many drinkers.

'I bet it smelled,' said another. 'I saw all the blood that poured out of his neck.'

Gideon laughed. 'It was messy and smelly, but not as bad as the dung I usually have to clear up.' He laughed and took a hefty slurp of ale before grasping his long lank hair and wiping his mouth with it.

Several of those around him burst into belly-laughs at this, much to his glee.

Hubert had assumed the manner of a vaguely interested traveller, taking up a position close enough to hear the man yet not too near to be considered as one that was over-keen to associate with him. He planned to observe and listen and then later, either here or at another tavern, actually make conversation with him.

'I'm thinking of giving up dung farming and taking up a new trade,' Gideon announced.

'What's that then, Gideon?'

'Executioner! I'm good at it, it seems, and it only takes a single blow and off the head rolls.' He drank more. 'I just need to practice hanging ordinary folk like you lot.'

There was more laughter before Gideon raised his hands and announced, 'That's it, friends. I'm going to add some piss for some other poor bugger to clean up.'

There was further laughter as he left, staggering to the door.

'The cursed fool; he may think he's the luckiest man in England, but it might be his luck to fall in the latrine,' someone muttered as soon as he had gone.

The smiles that had been so obvious as the ale was flowing disappeared.

'That wouldn't be any more than he deserved,' said another voice.

A bleary-eyed drinker, staring mournfully into his now empty tankard, belched loudly. 'Aye, and he was one that went fornicating where he shouldn't have done,' he said. 'That weren't right, what he did.'

'The murdering bastard,' said one of the customers who had supped from Gideon of Twyford's firkin.

'And yet you took his drink,' complained another drunkard.

'Aye, well, why wouldn't I?' the other returned.

'Because of this,' the loyal drunk replied, suddenly swinging a fist at the other and catching him on the temple.

A scuffle broke out and Hubert stepped back as several drinkers joined in, fists flying.

Few people noticed the hooded figure that had been drinking on his own in the corner. Hubert had noticed him, though, for the man had been watching the dung farmer almost as closely as he had. Hubert watched as he rose from his table, skirting the brawling men now rolling on the straw-strewn floor as others roared them on.

I shall give you a few moments' start, my friend, then I shall see why you are so interested in Gideon of Twyford, thought Hubert to himself.

The minstrels played while a pantler and his assistants began serving trenchers of bread for all, and finger bowls for every two people. Streams of serving women followed swiftly with salvers of cut meats, steaming pots and jugs of both wine and ale.

Three roast boars' heads were brought in on salvers, each surrounded by a ring of apples and with a crown of greenery. One was placed on the royal table and one each on the two long tables for the guests.

Then followed trays of venison, fowl and fish, vegetables and pots of various sauces, so that soon the hall was full of mouth-watering aromas.

As was to be expected, Bishop John de Stratford, as the host in his own palace, was first to formally start the proceedings. He shook a bell at his side and immediately the minstrels ceased playing. He stood and boomed out a greeting to His Majesty King Edward and Queen Philippa, and to Queen Isabella and to the Earl of March, and to those invited lords, ladies and knights. Then there was a more wordy speech made by Sir Roger Mortimer, a short acknowledgement by King Edward and various obsequious toasts made to the king and queen and the royal party by various adherents of Sir Roger from the floor.

Finally, the bishop said a grace in Latin and the feasting began. At a signal from the bishop, the musicians began to play again.

Despite the opulence of the feast and the copious amounts of wine that were being foisted upon him, Richard continued to be wary. From time to time he cast an eye at Sir Ranulf and the other judges, and also upon the royal table. He noted how Sir Roger Mortimer's attention was similarly diverted, his gaze moving around the hall as if trying to somehow glean information about the guests.

'What do you think of the Rhenish wine, Sir Richard?' asked Millicent de Berkeley, who was seated at his side.

'It is as fine as I have ever tasted, my lady.'

'It is from Bishop de Stratford's own cellar,' her husband, Sir John Maltravers, volunteered on Richard's other side. 'He is a fine cleric, you know. A most loyal priest.'

'I think most priests are loyal, Sir John,' Richard replied.

The knight looked at him askance. 'Do you really? It is not at all what I have heard. Take your own Archbishop of York, for instance.'

'Archbishop William Melton, Sir John? I'm not sure I understand you.'

Maltravers scrutinised Richard for a moment. 'Why, surely it is obvious. He appeared before the King's Bench two years ago because of his opposition to the government.'

'He was entirely acquitted of that matter, and as you know, he married His Majesty and Her Majesty afterwards.'

Maltravers shrugged. 'Perhaps he did, yet he may have had a part to play in the recent high treason by the Earl of Kent.'

Richard had himself had dealings with Archbishop Melton, including having saved his life in Pontefract. While not being a personal friend, he felt he should defend him. Noting how intently both Sir John and Lady Millicent were listening, he determined to be careful in his choice of words.

'I cannot believe —' he began. A sudden raised voice from further down the table caused him to pause. Sir Ranulf was angrily thumping the table with a fist and raising his voice in anger at something that either Thomas de Berkeley or his wife, Lady Margaret Mortimer, had said.

'A traitor? Never! And I'll not allow abuse of the law in my court.'

Lady Margaret patted his arm and, pointing to his cow horn, said something into it. It seemed to placate the judge, for he grunted and turned his attention to his wine while Baron Thomas de Berkeley leaned closer and talked in his other ear.

Ranulf should be careful not to react so quickly, Richard thought, convinced now that the guests had been seated between people who were quite deliberately trying to provoke a reaction and sound out loyalties.

He saw Ranulf glare at someone on the other side of the table. Richard leaned forward to reach for a piece of fruit, attempting to catch a glimpse of the person sitting opposite Ranulf. It was a younger man dressed in a simple brown tunic without an obvious badge of office or coat of arms. His hair was long and from that angle Richard could not properly see his features. The only conclusion he could come to was that he was perhaps a younger relative of the de Berkeleys or of Sir Roger Mortimer or some of his adherents. The fellow said something to Ranulf, receiving an angry glower and a grunt of dismissal from the judge in response.

Maintaining his own cool demeanour, Richard adroitly fended off further questions and was even able to turn the conversation round to Berkeley Castle and the final days of the late King Edward II. But Sir John Maltravers was equally skilled in the art of evasion, as was Millicent de Berkeley.

'I understand that you have a son, Sir Richard,' she said. 'I am sure your wife will be keen for your return to her and your boy.'

'Indeed, my lady. It is a great distance, so it will take —'

They were interrupted by a commotion from the other side of the table, almost underneath the minstrels' gallery. The sound of a wooden chair scraping backwards on the floor was followed by a strangled scream.

All eyes turned and people stood up to see what had happened. Even the royal party stood and looked on from behind the high table.

'It is Sir Jasper de Beausale!' someone cried.

As he stood, Richard saw a man staggering backwards, his hands clutching his throat as foam escaped from his mouth. Then he fell backwards onto the floor and started to convulse.

Chairs were pushed back and people gathered around the fallen knight.

'Fetch my physician!' called out Bishop John de Stratford. Immediately a servant burst through one of the doors, calling out to others in the bishop's staff to find the physician.

'Someone do something!' cried a lady kneeling beside the writhing man, whose face was turning purple. She was clearly his wife.

Moments later a bearded man came rushing in, carrying a leather sack. He quickly knelt by Sir Jasper and authoritatively ordered people to stand back to give him some air.

'This man is having a fit and he may have swallowed his tongue,' the physician said loudly.

He produced a flat piece of wood and, grasping the knight's lower jaw in one hand, pulled it down and proceeded to insert the wood into his mouth to depress the tongue.

It made no difference. The knight's body continued to writhe and shake, until with one final spasm it seemed to go floppy.

The physician bent over his chest and listened before gently closing Sir Jasper's eyelids.

Sir Roger Mortimer had left the high table and came to stand over the knight.

'What ails Sir Jasper de Beausale?' he demanded.

The physician stood and shook his head. 'Nothing, my lord. This man is dead.'

The lady kneeling by the dead knight started to wail.

7

Rather than returning to Winchester Castle, Sir Roger Mortimer and Queen Isabella had chosen to stay the night at the bishop's palace. Mortimer left Queen Isabella's bed during the night and made his way by the light of an oil lamp to the arranged meeting place, Bishop de Stratford's private chapel, which had been made available to him.

Candles were left burning beside the altar throughout the entire day and night for the bishop to observe a select number of the canonical hours. It was his custom to pray at vespers at sunset, lauds in the early morning, sext at noon and compline at the end of the day.

After the dramatic events of the evening, Sir Roger had told Stratford that he would celebrate lauds alone. The bishop understood only too well that that meant he was not to come to the chapel, for Mortimer had arranged to meet with someone — a person who would not be stopped by guards. It was not the first time such a meeting had been arranged by the Earl of March.

Sir Roger Mortimer was kneeling in prayer when he heard a footstep behind him. Despite the fact that he was expecting the visitor, he rose swiftly and spun round, ready for any attack. When one lived as he had done, the threat of assassination was ever-present, no matter how well guarded he was.

'Have no fear, my lord — it is I, as we arranged.' The voice was soft and had a somnolent quality to it. 'I have done all that you have commanded of me.'

'None saw you?'

'None when I acted, my lord. As you know, I can move in the shadows like no other.'

Mortimer nodded approvingly. 'Are you ready to undertake the rest of your mission? There must be no mistakes.' He went through exactly what he wanted doing, and what precisely would be the outcome.

The visitor smiled. 'I understand perfectly, my lord.'

'And you have no qualms about these deaths that you will bring about?'

'None, my lord. I have killed many. When I visited Naples, I learned that there are a multitude of ways that one may kill without a trace.' The visitor paused and gave an unpleasant smile. 'Look at my hands, my lord. Can you see even a drop of blood?'

Mortimer gave a guttural murmur of approval. 'That is impressive.'

'Yet I can leave the most obvious of signs when they are needed.'

'As you have just done?'

'Aye, and they will be discovered soon enough. You will be informed by others when the sun rises on this day, my lord.'

Mortimer smiled. 'You have done well, my friend. And you know what must be done and upon which day? This is most important, for the sentinel must have absolute evidence. Only then can the treachery and devilment become widely known.'

'I shall do it so that it cannot be concealed, unlike my own duplicity, which will be undetected. Have no fear, my lord, I shall do everything just as you have instructed.'

'Just ensure that the deaths cannot be traced back to me in any way.'

'They will be arranged to implicate those whom you have told me, my lord. Now, as for —?'

'Your reward? Fear not, it shall be as I promised. Greater, if all goes well. Now, go and Godspeed.'

When his minion had departed as silently as they had come, Mortimer returned to his kneeling position and resumed his prayers. The irony of his meeting in this place of worship was not lost on him, but for all that, he believed that God was on his side.

A rustling sound from the corridor behind made him pause and look over his shoulder. He smiled, realising it was just a draught in the corridor. There was no one there.

He finished his prayers and, picking up his flickering oil lamp, made his way back to his queen's bed. Tomorrow he had another important meeting which would put another part of his plan into action.

Hubert woke Richard just after cockcrow. The grey light of dawn shone through the frosted-up window of his room in the tavern.

'I thought you'd want to know, my lord. There's a head on a stake in front of the castle gate.'

Richard swung his legs out of his bed and rubbed the sleep from his eyes before standing to cross the room. 'Surely not Sir Edmund? Executing one of royal blood was bad enough, but to put his head on a spike on top of the Winchester Castle gate!'

'It's not above the gate, my lord, but outside it. And it's just on a simple stake driven into the ground.'

Richard peered through the window and saw a small crowd gathered near the castle gate. 'I see it, but it does not look like the earl's head.'

'No, my lord. It's the head of the man they got to swing the axe that severed it.'

Richard turned to stare at Hubert. He noticed the large bruise on the side of his head. 'How came you by that?'

Hubert looked embarrassed. 'I let my guard down, my lord. I am afraid that I failed in the task you gave me, for I had tracked Gideon of Twyford — whose head you see by the castle gate — to a tavern where he was spending money as if he had a bottomless purse. He was bragging about what he had done and how he had won his freedom by smiting off the Earl of Kent's head when no other would do so. He was telling all those who would listen and drink with him that he had found a new way of earning a living instead of farming dung.'

'Did you talk to him?'

'I was about to, my lord. He had left the tavern to relieve himself. I saw another man who was interested in him and he left a few moments after him.'

'A soldier or a traveller or a cleric of some sort?'

Hubert shrugged hopelessly. 'He was no soldier or guard, but he was a drinker. He was hooded, so I could not see his face.'

'Did you follow?'

'That was my intention, sir. But as soon as I got outside, two men attacked me.' He winced as he touched his bruised temple. 'That's what I meant when I said I let my guard down.'

'Was one of them this mysterious hooded man?'

'No, my lord. They were footpads, and not very good ones at that. They came at me with cudgels. I had my staff with me and quickly overcame them both. One has a broken nose and will walk bow-legged for a day or two, and the other is missing several teeth. I cracked their heads together and made them tell me why they attacked me. They were simple ruffians and said they had been paid to do so. They did not know the man, but he had given them a couple of coins to stand in the shadows outside the tavern and to deal with anyone who came out after him.'

'And are they in custody now?'

'No, my lord. I did not have time to summon anyone so I let them go, each with a kick to their backside. Then I searched for Gideon of Twyford and the hooded man. But there was no sign of them. It was only when I rose early this morning that I heard about the head on the pole and went to look and confirm that it was Gideon of Twyford. Then I came back here to tell you, my lord.'

Richard frowned. 'Yet the castle guards have not removed it, though I see there is one standing beside it, to keep the onlookers from disturbing it.' Richard stroked his chin. 'They are bound to have reported it, but they will be awaiting orders as to what to do. That order will not be given until Sir Roger Mortimer himself has heard of it, I would wager.'

'Do you want to see it yourself, my lord?'

'I do, as soon as I have washed and dressed.'

While Richard went about his ablutions, Hubert readied his clothes.

'Was the feast more to your liking than you expected, my lord?'

'It was cut short, Hubert. A knight called Sir Jasper Beausale had a fit and died. It upset Queen Philippa and King Edward, who declared the feast over. So, we were all dismissed. Of course, we were told by Sir Roger Mortimer to wait until the royal party were safely escorted from the hall.'

He described what had happened, including his suspicions that many of the guests like himself and Sir Ranulf Fermont had been seated between those who were aligned with Sir Roger Mortimer and Queen Isabella.

'This Sir Jasper, was he one such guest, my lord?'

'No, I am certain he is one who was in thrall to Mortimer. I was glad to leave the palace; I had lost my taste for the food and wine.'

'Then you would have been abroad in the city, as was I, my lord?'

'I was going to walk with Sir Ranulf, but I could not find him. I think he was angered by his conversation with Thomas de Berkeley or his wife, Lady Margaret Mortimer.'

'She is a Mortimer?'

'Sir Roger Mortimer's eldest daughter. As I said, I could not find Sir Ranulf, so I decided to walk back along by the southern city wall. As I passed St Swithun's I was greeted by another knight, who called out to me from the shadows. It was Sir William de Montagu, one of King Edward's staunchest friends. He is older than the king, but they have known each other all their lives, and last year he was sent as a special envoy to meet His Holiness Pope John at Avignon.'

'Was this meeting with Sir William contrived, my lord?'

'It was. We talked fleetingly of the events of this week and of the tragedy at the feast, but it was plain that he was testing me. He told me that he knew of the services I had performed for the late king and said that he acted for King Edward the Third. Indeed, he told me that it was King Edward's wish to convey to me his desire that I should be as loyal to him and be prepared to act for him in the same way should he ever have need of it.'

Richard finished his dressing by tying on his belt and adjusting his sheathed dagger. 'I told him I had always been loyal to the Crown and that the law of the land was of prime importance to me. Then I emphasised that above all I upheld justice in its truest sense.' He shrugged. 'And that was that. He shook my hand and replied that he would pass that answer back to His Majesty, who would be pleased to hear it. Then he strongly advised me to say nothing of the meeting before he disappeared into the shadows of another alley.'

Hubert blew through his lips. 'So, what happens now, my lord?'

'We are free to leave Winchester. We may travel home as soon as the city gates are opened.'

Hubert sighed. 'I for one will not be sad to leave this city.'

'We will be travelling part of the way along the Great North Road with Sir Ranulf Fermont and his servant.'

'Let us hope it is not too windy, my lord. We may have to shout for Sir Ranulf to hear us.'

'Indeed. But before we make ready to go home, let us first take a look at that head.'

It was an ugly sight when they walked to the castle gate. The crowd of onlookers, loafers, merchants and artisans for the main part, were staring at the grisly head upon the stake, which was a crude pole that looked to have been sharpened with a sword before being driven into the ground near the drawbridge to the castle.

Virtually everyone seemed to have an opinion. There was much speculation on the nature of the death of the Earl of Kent's executioner. There was also a good deal of anxiety and superstitious chatter about what this heralded.

Hubert had cleared a way through the crowd, announcing that Sir Richard Lee, Judge of the King's Northern Realm needed to pass. No one dared challenge Hubert's authoritative voice, including the young guard who stood by the staked head, yet studiously avoiding looking at it.

The crowd went silent as Richard inspected the stake and the head upon it. After a few moments, having seen all that he needed, Richard turned and signed for Hubert to clear a path for them back through the crowd. As they left, the whispers and murmurings started up again.

'It looks like the head was cut with a single blow,' Richard said to Hubert as they returned down the road towards the tavern.

'But where is the body, my lord?'

'Not close, I think,' Richard replied. 'Possibly it will be found in a ditch or secreted in some alleyway. Blood has dripped down the stake, yet there is none on the ground. He was killed elsewhere, and much of the blood has drained from the head. That means it was carried here with the stake and put here deliberately. But by whom? And why?'

'Are you going to investigate, my lord? Shall I start making enquiries?'

Richard gave a wry smile. 'I have no jurisdiction or authority to do so here, Hubert. It would be interesting to see what reaction this gruesome murder will evoke, but I doubt that we will be around to find out.'

'We are not waiting, my lord?'

'No. Like you, I will not be unhappy to leave Winchester. So much has happened that is distasteful and has shaken my faith in English justice. More than anything, I long to see Lady Wilhelmina and my son.'

8

Back at the tavern, sated with bread, a bowl of gruel and a mug of weak ale, Hubert packed their saddlebags, having arranged with the ostler to have their horses readied. Richard, meanwhile, kept watch through the window where he had a clear view of the castle gate. He saw half a dozen guards march towards the spiked head, under the orders of a captain. They had come prepared, for they carried a large basket into which the head was placed. Then, rather than entering the castle, they returned from whence they had come. Richard assumed it was from Wolvesey Castle, the Bishop's Palace.

'So, the executioner's head has been taken down and presumably someone in authority is going to inspect it,' Richard told Hubert.

They were finally about to depart when a priest hurried up to them.

'Sir Richard, I have a summons for you,' he said a little breathlessly, for he had been running. 'It is from His Grace, Bishop de Stratford.' He handed over a message bearing the Bishop of Winchester's seal. Richard broke it open and, unfolding the parchment, read it.

He whistled softly then nodded to the priest. 'Tell His Grace that I shall attend shortly. I shall ride there.'

'Will it be about the murder of Gideon of Twyford, my lord?' Hubert asked.

Richard shrugged his shoulders. 'I am not sure. It is not the bishop who wants to see me, but Sir Roger Mortimer.'

'The Earl of March himself?' Hubert asked, concern in his voice.

Richard nodded. 'His message says that he will not detain me long, so while I am there you should go and tell Sir Ranulf that we have been delayed.'

The summons to see the Earl of March sent a tingle of apprehension down Richard's spine, especially after the conversation he'd had the previous night with Sir William de Montagu. He wondered if they had been seen together, or overheard.

Bishop John de Stratford conducted Richard to his private office. Already feeling slightly anxious, he felt his heart pound harder when he saw that Queen Isabella was sitting behind the large desk. Her consort, the still-married Sir Roger Mortimer, was standing in the centre of the room.

'Your Majesty,' Richard said, immediately dropping into a bow before the king's mother and the widow of the late King Edward II.

Queen Isabella acknowledged him with a nod.

'Sir Roger,' he said, bowing again to the earl and receiving an abbreviated bow in return.

'That will be all, John,' said Sir Roger, dismissing the Bishop of Winchester from his own office. 'We need to talk to Sir Richard in private.'

Richard did not see how the bishop reacted, but he heard the door close behind him.

'You wished to see me, my lord,' he said, wondering if they were going to ask him to investigate the murder of the executioner, Gideon of Twyford, or perhaps look into Sir Jasper de Beausale's death at the feast.

'*We* wish to see you!' said Queen Isabella emphatically.

'My apologies, Your Majesty,' Richard said hurriedly. 'Is there some service I can do you?'

Sir Roger Mortimer smiled. 'There is a service we ask of you, Sir Richard. We are aware that you are a Sergeant-at-Law and the King's Judge of his Northern Realm. You have done service for the Crown before and we understand that you have certain … abilities.'

'I am a lawyer and a dispenser of the law, my lord.'

'And a seeker of the truth and one who catches those guilty of crimes and treason,' Queen Isabella said, her mouth curving into a smile that, despite himself, Richard found quite alluring. And yet past experience had taught him that attractive women could also be capable of murder.

'I uphold the law of the land, Your Majesty.'

'Well said, Richard,' said Mortimer, adopting a friendly tone and dropping the use of his title.

Is he being genuinely friendly or does he intend to put me off my guard? Richard thought. *I must remain vigilant.*

'As you are only too aware, treachery and treason have taken root in England,' Mortimer went on. 'His Majesty has had no alternative than to root it out wherever it presents itself. This we have seen this past week.'

Richard made no reply, but instead bobbed his head in slight acknowledgement.

'There is evil in the land, Richard, and we must not allow it to thrive. At the Earl of Kent's trial we heard his signed confession, in which he stated that he had dealings with those who practise the Dark Arts and who raised a demon to reveal secrets.'

'Secrets that were lies,' Queen Isabella interjected.

'Nevertheless, this demon's message twisted and turned the earl's mind and made him commit treason against King Edward,' continued Mortimer. 'For that great sin, Kent forfeited his life.'

'What is it you require of me, my lord?'

'We must find this friar who delivered the message from the Devil.'

'Do you know where he was from, my lord? What order he belonged to? Do you have any clues?'

'He was from the North, from His Majesty's Northern realm.'

'How do you know this, my lord?'

'He revealed it to the Earl of Kent.'

'But I do not recollect that being mentioned in his confession.'

'Not in his written confession, but in his verbal one. I was one of his interrogators. He said that the friar was from a holy house in Yorkshire, with rich patrons.'

'And this house is where exactly?'

Sir Roger held his hands up. 'I regret bitterly that I did not follow up on this question. I and my fellow interrogators wished to know the details of the earl's treasonous crimes.'

'So now you can see why we summoned you here, Sir Richard,' said the queen, smiling once again. 'It is in your area of jurisdiction that we must find this friar.'

'If there is one, there may be many,' said Mortimer. 'Witchcraft and sorcery are abominations and could do untold damage to the royal house and to the country.'

'So, you want me to seek this monk?'

'We wish you to be watchful, and if you find any evidence of anyone raising demons or practising the Dark Arts then you must urgently notify us. And then we must act to protect the throne and the land.'

'You wish me to make an arrest, my lord?'

'Not exactly. We wish you to simply be vigilant. We do not want to act in haste, so if you discover any evidence of anyone practising witchcraft or the Dark Arts then send a messenger to us, here in Winchester.'

'I have had enough betrayal in my life,' Queen Isabella added. 'My husband, the late King Edward, betrayed me with — his favourites.'

'First the traitor Piers Gaveston and then with Hugh le Despenser, both of whom are mercifully no longer a threat,' Sir Roger added by way of explanation.

Richard had met both men and had actually saved the life of Piers Gaveston. He suppressed a shudder as he recalled how both had been so barbarically executed. Gaveston had been found guilty of treason by the Earl of Arundel, among others, and then summarily executed by being run through and then beheaded by two Welsh soldiers. Hugh le Despenser had been hung, drawn and quartered, upon the orders of Mortimer and Queen Isabella.

The queen was speaking again. 'And I have been personally betrayed by women whom I had counted as friends and elevated. Women like Lady Isabella de Vesci.'

Richard knew who she was talking about. Lady Isabella de Vesci was a member of the Beaumont family and had married into the de Vesci family. She had been a courtier but had taken herself home to the north after the Scottish wars, when Mortimer and Queen Isabella had opted for peace by signing the Treaty of Northampton with Robert the Bruce, King of the Scots. The result had been that the Beaumonts lost a considerable amount of land on the Scottish Borders as part of the settlement.

Mortimer clapped his hands, indicating that the interview was drawing to a close. 'So, Richard, you are to be our eyes and ears in the North. And if you discover anything, you must inform us and await further instruction.'

'I will do my utmost to uphold the law and deal with evil wherever I find it, my lord.'

They did not appear to be concerned about the murder of Gideon of Twyford. Nor were they interested in the death of Sir Jasper de Beausale. These matters were obviously of little importance to them.

Richard bowed and as they dismissed him he backed up to the door and let himself out. John de Stratford was waiting to re-enter. Richard had little doubt that the bishop had been listening intently at the door.

Hubert rode to the tavern where Richard had told him that Sir Ranulf was staying. He was surprised to find two armed guards standing on either side of the tavern door. A woman was sitting on an empty barrel outside, weeping noisily. The innkeeper, in a leather apron, was trying to comfort her.

'What is the matter?' Hubert asked, dismounting and leading his horse by the reins to tether it.

'You, fellow, be off with you!' said one of the guards. 'No one's coming in here today.'

Hubert bristled and stood his ground. 'And you, fellow, take care with your manners, if you know what's good for you. I am Hubert of Loxley, Sir Richard Lee's assistant. He is Judge of His Majesty's Northern Realm and I am here under his orders to see Sir Ranulf Fermont.'

The woman turned her head at mention of the name then burst into a further flood of tears.

The guard who had spoken looked confused and turned to the older guard standing on the other side of the door.

'We didn't know who you were, sir,' the older one said. 'We are waiting here until we receive further orders.'

'Who is your captain?'

'We are the Earl of March's men, sir. We were called by the night watch, who were alerted by the landlord here. You won't be talking to Sir Ranulf, that's for sure.'

Hubert eyed him suspiciously. 'Why, what has happened?'

The landlord was a middle-aged fellow with bowed legs. He hobbled across and looked up at Hubert. 'Murder and robbery, sir. Both of them. Sir Ranulf and his servant.'

'I'd better take a look,' said Hubert.

The guards let the landlord pass and Hubert followed. They went along a short corridor with several doors until they faced the one at the end.

'It's my best room, sir. Sir Ranulf demanded that. Neither he nor his servant came down to break their fast, so I knocked and … and found them, sir.'

The landlord opened the door to reveal the body of a young servant. He was lying on his back at the foot of the bed. A deep gash showed where his throat had been slit. Sprawled on the bed was the body of Sir Ranulf Fermont. His face was fixed in a look of horror, and one eye socket was a gory mess. The instrument that had gouged his eye out was obvious. His cow horn was protruding from his mouth, where it had been shoved down his throat. Blood and stomach contents had spilled out of the horn.

A breeze from a half-open window made some of the hairs in the judge's blood-caked beard move back and forth.

'It looks like the murderer came and went through that window,' Hubert said, more to himself than to the landlord. 'Undoubtedly in the middle of the night as they both slept.'

There was the noise of boots on the stairs, and a moment later a captain of the guard bearing the royal livery entered.

'The guard told me who you are, Hubert of Loxley, but you can go now. I am instructed by Sir Roger Mortimer, the Earl of March to deal with this.'

Hubert was about to remonstrate, but then he reconsidered. To antagonise one of Sir Roger's men, especially one that wore the royal livery, did not seem a good idea. He had no wish to cause trouble for Sir Richard. Besides, he was keen to leave Winchester and head home to the arms of his wife and children.

But he did not relish the prospect of telling Sir Richard the gruesome news.

9

Darrington Manor, Yorkshire, 29 March 1330

Lady Isabella de Vesci stared in horror at her brother, Lewis de Beaumont, the Bishop of Durham. 'I do not believe it! King Edward's uncle has been executed? Have Mortimer and Queen Isabella no shame?'

'They have no shame, no heart and no soul if this is true,' the bishop said, leaning forward and holding his head in his hands.

They were sitting in the solar of Lady de Vesci's manor house at Darrington, a few miles from Pontefract. Each had a goblet of wine, as did the young emissary who had travelled from Winchester to bring them the news.

He had described the Earl of Kent's arrest, trial and execution, and the subsequent feast that was held in Bishop John de Stratford's palace. Lady Isabella and her brother had listened in horrified astonishment as he had also told them of the discovery of the severed head of the latrine cleaner who had wielded the execution axe.

Their disbelief was heightened further when they were told of the murder of Sir Ranulf Fermont and his servant in the tavern where they had been staying.

'It makes no sense,' said the bishop. 'Sir Ranulf was not associated with any faction opposed to Queen Isabella and Sir Roger Mortimer, so why kill him?'

'His murder may be unrelated to the execution of the Earl of Kent,' said the emissary. 'It may have been simple theft and murder.'

'Theft and murder are never simple,' the bishop remarked, taking a hefty mouthful of his wine.

'Indeed not, my lord bishop. I have no more information than this. I do not know if his murder was investigated, as I was despatched to inform you and also the Earl of Lancaster.'

'He is staying in Pontefract Castle, so you will not have far to travel now,' said Lady de Vesci.

The emissary sipped his wine. 'I must not tarry too long, as I have also been instructed to warn others, including His Grace Archbishop Melton.'

'You must eat with us first,' Lady Isabella replied, determined to be hospitable despite the anxiety she felt.

'I thank you, but I have supped recently and I must discharge my duties so that you can all be prepared for any move against you.'

Bishop Lewis frowned. 'It is a pity that we and the Earl of Lancaster are infirm and ill-prepared for any long journey if we must flee.'

Lady de Vesci slapped her hands together irritably. 'We cannot even seek help beyond the border in Scotland after Mortimer and Isabella made that disastrous Treaty of Northampton, which caused us to lose our lands there. The scheming mongrel has effectively trapped us here in the North, unless Lancaster is able to lead an army...'

'He can barely see!' said the bishop sharply. 'He could not lead an army, although he is the most powerful opponent of Mortimer, and cousin to King Edward the Second.' He beat his brow with a fist. 'It is as if we have been cursed and demons have been set to work upon us.'

The emissary sighed and set down his goblet. 'There is something else that you must be aware of. The Earl of Kent in his confession said that a friar told him that he had raised a demon, which said that his brother, King Edward the Second, still lived. That is apparently the reason that Sir Roger Mortimer had him arrested. It is claimed that he had dealings with a demon and planned to attack Berkeley Castle to rescue his brother. That was an act of treason against our king.'

Both Lady Isabella and the Bishop of Durham stared at the emissary in horror.

'Then we are undone!' the bishop exclaimed. 'We are truly all in danger and must be prepared for anything.'

Sister Odelina lay on the cot in her cell at Cawthorne Priory. She was exhausted and had closed the shutter on the high overhead window so that she could lie in the dark. She had prayed several times throughout the day, then had dripped molten candle wax into a bowl of water to see the shapes that her angel had sent her. She had covered the bowl with the silk veil that she had worn when she first entered the priory as a child. It was the only piece of clothing that linked her with the life that she barely remembered.

She was now a woman of thirty-six years and had been brought up in the nunnery section of the priory before becoming first a lay sister and then a nun at the age of eighteen.

Although she had seen her angel since she was a girl, she had kept her secret from most of the nuns. She had confided in Sister Griselda, though, who was now the Mother Superior. Her angel visited her often in the night and gave her messages. Then the miracle occurred, which changed her life forever.

When she became pregnant by her angel and the nuns wanted to beat her to make her tell the name of the lay brother or the monk who had planted his seed within her womb, it was Sister Griselda who saved her.

Bless Griselda, her friend, her Mother Superior. The only one who believed her. She it was who gave her the birth girdle, the ten-foot-long roll of sheepskin parchment, made up of squares sewn together and inscribed with prayers and images of angels and Saints Margaret and Veronica. It would offer divine assistance when her time came.

The nuns had watched over her as her belly swelled over all those months. They castigated her for her wickedness, implored her to confess, and told her that eternal damnation would come to her.

But she remained resolute despite them and proclaimed her virginity in the face of their recriminations and accusations. Left alone in the cell that they locked her in, visited only by Sister Griselda, she read the prayers on her birth girdle and called upon her angel.

Then when her labour started and she bound the birth girdle around her huge belly, they crept back in fear as she called upon her angel and told them that she was being watched over. They left her in the cell and when they had come back — after her crying and labour were over — they had seen the miracle. The angel had taken the child from her, leaving no blood, no sign of pregnancy at all.

She had insisted upon remaining in that cell from then onwards rather than returning to the dormitory, or joining the senior nuns in their individual cells in the dorter corridor. Although only Mother Griselda knew it, it was in that cell that her angel talked to her in the night, usually after matins. It had been her angel who had told her that, to protect herself from evil, she had to become an anchoress.

It was from then that she had been able to heal others, by wrapping her birth girdle around the parts of the body that were ailing the person. They came from far and near, the great and the good and the mighty.

Sister Odelina would heal them, and to special visitors she would give messages from her angel.

'Sister Odelina,' came the voice of Sister Patience from the other side of the cell wall. 'I have food and fresh milk for you.'

The sound of scraping metal made her wince, as so many noises did, and a tiny ray of light from outside shone through the darkness as the grille in the corner of the cell opened.

A mug was shoved through, and then a plate with bread and cheese.

'Thank you, Patience.'

'Sister Odelina, may I ask, have you had any messages from your angel for me?'

Sister Odelina smiled in the darkness. She liked the young lay sister who had been given the daily job of emptying her chamber pot and bringing her sustenance, and who was always so deferential and timid.

'Bless you, Patience. Yes, I was told that you have been diligent and good and that light shines around you.'

Patience was about twenty years old, older than she herself had been when she had become a nun. But unlike so many others who wanted to become nuns and devote themselves to the Lord, Patience was content to remain a lay sister. She felt no need to do any more with her life than she already did.

Sister Odelina smiled as the young woman thanked her effusively. The grille slid closed and she heard the lay sister's footsteps receding.

She shivered in the darkness. It was not merely because the cell was cold, but because of the message that her angel had actually given her. His voice had come to her in the night, just as it had done before — whispering so that only she could hear his words.

'Death is coming to Cawthorne. Beware of treachery.'

Sister Odelina crossed herself at the thought of yet more death.

At Pontefract Castle Henry of Lancaster was in a state of turmoil. Grief, shock and anger were all mixed with disbelief.

The young emissary had brought him the news that his cousin, Edmund of Woodstock, had been executed.

'I wish I could see you more clearly, but I fear that my eyes are getting worse.'

'Can no physic help you, my lord?'

'I have tried everything that my physician and apothecary have given me. The only thing that helps is the intercession of a local anchoress and the touch of a holy object, a birth girdle.'

The emissary made the sign of the cross. 'The help of the divine surely supersedes that of mortal men and their physic.'

'Yet now with the news that you have brought me this day, I fear that my ears are failing me, too.'

The details had stunned him.

'I had tried to warn Sir Edmund about going to Winchester, but he thought that as he was an uncle to King Edward he was protected. He is — was — of royal blood. As am I, for I was cousin to his father.'

The emissary informed him of the murder of the executioner and of Sir Ranulf Fermont and his servant. Through it all the earl sat staring into the blazing fire in the huge fireplace.

'Sir Ranulf Fermont was a judge of impeccable character and wisdom. Everyone who met him knew that booming voice of his because of his deafness. He always carried a cow horn to listen through.'

Suddenly he rose from his chair and crossed swiftly to the fireplace. Picking up a poker he attacked with some vehemence the burning logs, stirring up flames and causing great flumes of smoke and red embers to shoot up the chimney.

'I will have to visit my anchoress again, although she is walled up forever so I cannot be touched by her. The prior told me that when next I go he will try to help with their other holy relic.'

'A relic, my lord?'

'The finger of Saint Gilbert. It is holy, for he anointed Saint Thomas Becket with it when they were both alive. Ever since it has had a miraculous effect, so I am told, on those with disorders of the head or the eyes.'

The young emissary cleared his throat. 'I am not familiar with this saint, my lord.'

'Are you not, indeed? Why, of all the saints his is the only English order. Cawthorne Priory and Watton Priory in the East Riding are the two main houses of his order in Yorkshire.'

'And I must needs visit York to seek out and inform Archbishop Melton of this tragedy.'

'It is a long ride from here to York. You had best stay the night here.'

'I thank you, my lord, but the sooner I discharge the tasks I have been sent on, the better. I will sleep only when these matters have been passed on to those who may yet be able to do something to save the country.'

'Which makes it all the more important that I visit my anchoress to help my vision, if I have to go into battle against Mortimer.'

With a final thrust of the poker as if it were a sword and the log his enemy, he thrust hard, cleaving it in two to create a further shower of sparks.

'I swear that I will bring this traitor, this murderer of those of royal blood, to justice.'

The emissary stood and bowed. 'If I may take my leave of you, my lord, I shall travel to York.'

'Godspeed! And may God help us all.'

It was late when the killer finally made it to bed. All the people that needed to be seen and talked to had been contacted and the necessary tasks completed.

Or rather, all the tasks so far. This was just the beginning, but it would mean the end for so many.

And for one victim, death would not only be painful, but prolonged.

10

Sandal Castle, Wakefield

Sir Thomas Deyville, the Steward of the Manor of Wakefield and of Sandal Castle, was in an unusually good mood, despite being laid up with another attack of podagra. His right foot was heavily wrapped in linen.

He lay on his large bed beside the narrow window of his chamber on the third floor of the North Tower of the keep.

Still subject to episodic melancholia after the sudden death of his wife, the Lady Alecia, three years previously, he was prone to throw mugs, bowls or flasks when events or situations caused his ire to rise. Yet there were two things that could be guaranteed to soothe him.

The first was his grandson, young Digby Lee, who was Richard and Wilhelmina's three-year-old son.

The second was music. He had always found it soothing, especially since Lady Alecia had been an accomplished harpist herself. They always had minstrels whenever they entertained, but since her demise the minstrels' gallery had remained empty, and no one dared to sing or whistle within earshot of him.

However, Digby's attempts to beat anything that resembled a drum would send Sir Thomas into fits of laughter, even the unmelodic noise that currently ensued.

'Don't stop him, Wilhelmina,' he said now as his mother was about to take the goblet that Digby was bashing against a bedpan in Sir Thomas's bedroom. 'The boy is showing he has strength. He will break nothing there. Let him beat away.'

Wilhelmina shook her head. 'I am sorry, Father, but it is my head I am concerned about. The noise is like to give me a headache.'

She gently eased the goblet from her son's hand, provoking tears and a few seconds of wailing before Richard stopped Digby's cries by lifting him into the air three times in rapid succession. The cries turned to laughter.

'Again! Again! Again!' Digby cried.

'Later, my son,' Richard said, kissing him and handing him to Wilhelmina. 'I have to talk to your grandfather before I ride to Wakefield.'

Sir Thomas reached up to tousle the boy's golden locks and gave him a smile as Wilhelmina left the bedchamber. Richard watched him and as he expected, the moment Wilhelmina and young Digby departed, any semblance of good humour disappeared from his father-in-law's demeanour.

'How goes the podagra, Sir Thomas?' Richard ventured.

'It is better than it was, but still troubles me greatly. I cannot walk or put my foot to the ground.'

'Is Doctor Brandon Flynn still attending you?'

Sir Thomas harrumphed. 'Twice a week, to bleed me and to bring a fresh supply of that foul-tasting concoction he makes up for me.' He pointed to a small flask beside a jug of water and an empty goblet. 'It's made from the root of a plant called the autumn crocus or meadow saffron or some such.'

'So something is helping?'

Sir Thomas shrugged. 'Maybe, but I'm sure it would help more if he hadn't told Wilfred to instruct the other servants that I am not to have any ale. He claims it makes my foot swell up like this.' He waved his hand irritably. 'But enough of my malady! From what my daughter has told me, things have taken a decidedly unpleasant turn in the country. Sit down and tell me, my boy.'

Richard drew a chair up to the bedside of his father-in-law. Much had changed in the eight years since he had come to Wakefield, when he was appointed as Circuit Judge of the King's Northern Realm by King Edward II of Caernarfon himself. Prior to this the Wakefield Manor Court had been held by Sir Thomas Deyville, who had a very different idea about justice to Richard. As Sir Thomas was not versed in the law he had dispensed what he considered to be appropriate sentences, although they had little legal precedent.

Things had not been easy between them in those early days, as Sir Thomas did not appreciate Richard assuming control of the Manor Court. He thought that his judgements were overly lenient, and they had a stormy beginning to their relationship. That was not eased by the fact that Sir Thomas and Lady Alecia had a comely daughter in Wilhelmina. Sir Thomas adopted an aggressively protective attitude as it became clear that the young couple were falling in love. Lady Alecia recognised their feelings and blessed the courtship, which softened Sir Thomas's attitude. Eventually, they forged a good and mutually respectful relationship.

Wilhelmina had travelled with Digby from their manor house in Durkar ahead of Richard, who had several affairs to deal with before he could leave.

'Wilhelmina has told you that Edmund of Woodstock, the Earl of Kent was beheaded outside Winchester Castle? That happened after I sent you my letter.'

'Aye, upon the orders of Sir Roger Mortimer, the Lord of Wigmore. But she says it was with the king's agreement.'

'It was made clear that the execution was with the king's authority.'

Sir Thomas harrumphed. 'Mortimer is too powerful by half.'

'He has given himself more titles and now likes to be addressed as the Earl of March.'

'And he is an adulterer with the late king's wife, Queen Isabella.' Sir Thomas could not keep the tone of disapproval from his voice. 'It is a scandal; she is young King Edward's mother!'

'There has been more villainy than that, Sir Thomas,' Richard said, using his father-in-law's title with respect. 'Sir Ranulf Fermont was murdered at the tavern where he was staying. The landlord let Hubert see the bodies of both Sir Ranulf and his servant, but then a captain of the guard came and told him that he and his men were to deal with it. So I was not given any opportunity to investigate. After everything that had gone before, we had no choice but to leave Winchester and return to Wakefield.'

'What of his family? Were they notified?'

'Sir Ranulf was a widower who lived with his sister. I paid a visit to their manor house in Lincoln on our way here to express my sympathies. She is a capable woman, and I have no doubt that she will be able to look after the estate.'

When he and Hubert had arrived at Sir Ranulf's manor house, Richard was not surprised to find the lady in a considerable state of distress, yet she was able to tell him that King Edward was going to arrange for Sir Ranulf's body to be brought back to the manor.

Sir Thomas harrumphed again. 'And Wilhelmina said something about the Earl of Kent's executioner?'

'They could not find anyone willing to perform the act, apart from this fellow who was himself condemned to death. He agreed to wield the axe in exchange for a pardon. He was also murdered — beheaded — but we do not know by whom.'

'Some pardon he received!'

'There is yet more, Sir Thomas. On the morning we left Winchester, I was summoned to see Sir Roger Mortimer and Queen Isabella. They want me to be their eyes and ears in the North.'

Sir Thomas thumped a fist into his palm. 'They want you to be their minion?'

Richard recounted the interview. He also told Sir Thomas of the Earl of Kent's confession that had been read out before the assembly.

'Sir Roger Mortimer said that Edmund of Woodstock had confessed that the friar who had raised a demon came from a holy house in this part of the realm. He did not know which one, and regretted that he had not pressed the earl for that information. But it is a holy house with wealthy patrons. They want me to be watchful, and if I discover any sorcery or witchcraft I am to inform them.'

'Sorcery? So, what do you plan to do, Richard?'

Richard shrugged his shoulders. 'I was not given a command to investigate this, just to keep my eyes and ears open. I do not relish being their instrument, so I will not actively do anything.'

'Are they working on the king's behalf? Or could, dare I venture to say it, they have ambitions to seize the throne from King Edward? As happened with the late King Edward the Second?'

Richard did not tell Sir Thomas about the clandestine talk he'd had with Sir William de Montagu. He had too many questions, which he had not resolved in his mind during the long cold journey back to Wakefield.

'Well, you will find that there is much work awaiting you when you go to the court,' said Sir Thomas. 'Wilfred my head servant has been notified regularly by the court clerk, John of Flanshaw, and he has a list of cases awaiting you in the Rolls Office in the Moot Hall.'

'I will find out soon enough,' Richard replied. 'I have sent one of my grooms from Durkar Manor to tell him that I will hold the next court session at one o'clock today.'

Later that morning Richard and Hubert crossed the drawbridge of Sandal Castle and rode down the hill through the village of Sandal Magna on their way to Wakefield.

'It is good to be home, my lord,' said Hubert as they took the undulating trail, skirting round oxcarts and wagons pulled by nags of varying age and health, and shepherds and swineherds conveying their livestock to market.

'Beatrice and your boys must have been pleased to see you, Hubert.'

'That they were, my lord. Dickon, my eldest, is already teaching his brothers how to fight, and all of them try to waylay me whenever they may.'

Richard laughed. 'My Digby looks set to become a musician, or a drummer at the very least. He amuses my father-in-law, which is no small task.'

'Is Sir Thomas any better, my lord?'

'Barely. In addition to his melancholia, his podagra prevents him from walking. And Doctor Flynn has ordered that he must not drink ale.'

Hubert sucked air in between his lips. 'Why, that last alone would make a man ill, surely, my lord?'

They laughed as they passed the village fishpond and then rode by cultivated lands, divided up into ridges and furrows, upon which several smock-clad peasants could be seen working. Beyond that could be seen the half-wooded Great Park, which was famously well stocked with deer, partridges and boar.

'It is a pity that Sir Thomas cannot ride his horse and get out to smell this good air,' Hubert said, breathing in deeply and then sighing contentedly.

He nodded to the Great Park. 'And more a pity that he cannot go hunting. Shooting one's own food is one of the finest ways to build an appetite for life.' He pointed ahead to the River Calder. 'Even catching a few fish would help.'

'Unfortunately, he just lies abed and waits for Doctor Flynn to bleed him and chastise him for not taking enough of his medicine. He worries about the Manor of Wakefield.'

Sandal Castle was the centre of the Manor of Wakefield, which extended for thirty miles or so across the country from east to west. With twelve graveships and almost one hundred and twenty towns, villages and hamlets, there was a considerable amount of overseeing necessary. All that administration nominally fell into the hands of Sir Thomas as the Steward of Sandal Castle, but in reality much of it was done by Wilfred, his head servant, under the guidance of Richard. And when he was away from home, Wilhelmina helped, as had her mother, Lady Alecia, before her.

Hubert shook his head. 'I would far rather assist you in the court or crack a head or two, like those two footpads who attacked me outside the tavern in Winchester.'

'That bump on your head has gone down well,' remarked Richard. 'I can no longer see the bruise.'

Hubert tapped his chest. 'My arrowhead protects me and it makes wounds heal quickly, my lord. A pity it doesn't make me feel any better for not preventing the murder of the Earl of Kent's executioner, Gideon of Twyford.'

They crossed the bridge over the river and entered the town by the Kirkgate, the southernmost of the three town gates.

'I feel bad that I could do nothing to stop the murders of Sir Ranulf and his servant, and that I could do nothing to discover their murderer,' said Richard. 'That on top of the execution of the Earl of Kent...'

He did not finish his sentence, but Hubert understood how his master felt.

They joined the throng that was making its way from the gate up through the street towards the town.

'But come, Hubert, let us not get too melancholic. At least here in Wakefield we may be free to dispense the king's justice.'

'And just listen to that tumult from the market,' Hubert said. 'Why, it is music to my ears. Mayhap we should bring Sir Thomas to hear the good folk of Wakefield.'

Richard smiled. 'This morning's work will be about reading whatever John of Flanshaw has prepared. It seems that most of the cases concern disputes over money, land or debts. The court will be held at one o'clock. So, why don't you join me then? In the meantime, have a look at the market and listen out for what is the news in town.'

Hubert nodded. 'I will, my lord. Although news from Winchester will not have reached here yet. Should I tell people about it?'

'It is merely a matter of time before official news arrives. If you are asked, you can merely give the facts that the Earl of Kent was tried in Winchester for high treason, found guilty and executed. It would be better not to express any opinion about it.'

'Even that will spread around the town by the end of the day.'

Richard nodded. 'I do not like it any more than you, Hubert. But it is not our duty to spread the news or to foment opinion.'

11

Wakefield was an ancient town built by the Saxons on a limestone ridge that sloped down to the River Calder. It was surrounded by a number of villages that had actually been Viking settlements. It was quite a prosperous town and not without its own charm. Indeed, throughout the north of the land it was called the 'Merrie Town', probably because it boasted several hostelries and bawdy houses.

Richard and Hubert left the Kirkgate tollgate and followed the road up the steep hill to the Birch Hill, where it met the other three main roads. Within this area there was a pond, a market cross and a large circular area called the Bull Ring. This was so named because bull- and bear-baiting regularly took place there on fair days.

On market days such as this, the whole area was covered in stalls and booths, temporary animal pens for the cattle and sheep that were driven for miles around to fetch the best prices they could for their owners. Accordingly, the streets were bustling with people.

But it was also the court day, and all who had dealings with the court were obliged to attend.

They made their way up the road, which was deeply rutted by oxcarts and pack-horses. On either side there were gabled wooden houses with roofs of thatch or reeds, and crude wattle and daub dwellings, most with undercrofts for animals and supplies. Dung heaps and refuse of all kinds had to be negotiated along with the flocks of animals, carts, donkeys and townsfolk alike.

Not far from the Bull Ring was the Tolbooth, and close to it was the Moot Hall where the Manor Court was held. As they crested the hill they could see the Church of All Saints with its mighty spire.

The Wodehalle, as the Moot Hall was known locally, was a large timber-framed building capable of holding up to two hundred people. It had been built a century before by William de Warenne, the fifth Earl of Surrey. Since then the Lords of the Manor of Wakefield and their appointed stewards used it for the various types of court heard throughout the year. Above its doors was the emblem of the de Warenne family, and above that was a small sundial. A stream of people were passing the main door, but they soon stood to one side at the sound of the horses. A young ostler was already waiting for them to arrive. He rushed forward as Richard and Hubert dismounted and led their mounts away to the nearby stable beyond the Tolbooth, where prisoners and those awaiting trial were held.

Hubert bowed and took his leave of Richard to mingle with the market crowd and pick up whatever local gossip he could.

'The Lord be with you, Sir Richard,' said a voice near the door of the Moot Hall.

Richard turned and saw a Franciscan friar dressed in a travel-worn grey habit of his order, standing with his hands pressed together. At his feet, almost a symbol of his mendicant order, was a bowl containing a few coins. 'I pray that you will be merciful in your deliberations in the court today. Remember that the Good Book tells us that there will be more joy over one sinner who repents than over ninety and nine just persons that need not repentance.'

'Good day, Friar Simon,' Richard replied. 'Fear not, as I dispense the king's justice and will be ever mindful of the teachings of the Bible.'

The friar, a well-built fellow in his late thirties, was well known in Wakefield and the surrounding villages and hamlets. He had a broken nose and was missing half an ear, thanks to his life as a soldier and a brawler before he became a friar of the Franciscan Order. He always stationed himself by the Moot Hall in advance of Richard's arrival and was ever-present in the court session, where he could be seen praying for whichever miscreant was currently being tried. Richard was all too aware that although he prayed for everyone, those whose relatives had tossed money into his bowl before he entered the court received both a longer and a more dramatic offering to the Lord.

'That is all I could hope for, Sir Richard,' the friar said, picking up his bowl. 'I shall see if I can find sinners among those in the market or the hostelries, and I shall see you in the court hall later.'

Richard watched the friar amble off, making the sign of the cross at passers-by as he went. With a smile, Richard entered the Moot Hall.

A long corridor led to a lockable room called the Rolls Office, which was furnished with a large desk and chair and several stools. Taking up a corner of the room was a large locked chest with numerous pigeon holes, containing the Manor of Wakefield court rolls. Dating back to 1274 and written in a mix of English and Latin on fine vellum scrolls, they recorded all of the dealings of the Manor Court.

John of Flanshaw, the town bailiff and the main officer of the court, was sitting at the desk writing on vellum when Richard opened the door.

'Ah, Sir Richard, welcome back, sir. I hope that the deliberations of the parliament were a success and that your journey home was not too arduous?'

'It was not an easy time, Master John. You have not heard, but the Earl of Kent was tried in the Great Hall of Winchester Castle and found guilty of treason. He was executed in front of the castle by an ex-criminal, who was himself murdered shortly after.'

The bailiff sat with his quill in his hand and stared at Richard in disbelief. 'But … but the Earl of Kent is — or was — of royal blood.'

'He was the late King Edward's younger half-brother and therefore uncle to King Edward the Third. That is correct.'

'But treason, sir? Surely not?'

'That was the finding of the trial, but I care not to comment further as I was neither involved in the investigation nor in the proceedings. Suffice to say that I am doubtful that true justice was served that day. I hope that we can do better here in Wakefield.'

The bailiff stared at him for a moment then rapidly nodded his head. 'Of course, Sir Richard. I was just making out the list of the court proceedings,' he said, replacing the quill in the holder beside the large pewter inkpot. He was a well-fed man in his late thirties with porcine eyes and a square-cut black beard flecked with grey. Richard knew him to be a stickler for routine, an able court clerk, and an efficient bailiff. Picking up a pounce pot containing ground-up cuttlefish bones, he sprinkled the powder on his list, tapped the vellum and then blew the loose particles away. 'It will dry in a moment, sir.'

Finally, in the obsessive manner that so amused Richard and which was characteristic of John, he straightened the vellum on the desk and stood to vacate the chair for Richard.

'A goodly crowd seems to be attending the market, and I had a proclamation made at cockcrow and then again at ten bells. In addition, the town constables have ensured that all the reeves know and they will have instructed all with business before the court to attend. The court shall be in session when the bell of the Church of All Saints sounds one o'clock.'

Richard nodded as he took his seat and placed his saddlebag by the side of the desk. Opening it, he took out his gavel and his coif, both of which he placed on the desk beside the documents.

'Then let us see what lies ahead of us in court today,' he said, picking up the list.

Hubert ambled around the market stalls, enjoying being back in the town. Most folk knew the tall assistant to Sir Richard Lee. Those who had never been in trouble with the court were happy to pass the time with him, offering him their produce for free, be that apples, pies or sticks of liquorice root. Those who had cause to fear the law or who had been dealt with in the court tended to give him a wide berth. Hubert was shrewd enough to recognise both types of people.

Amid all the clamour he heard the cries of costermongers and peddlers, calling out their wares, and of the various mountebanks standing upon the benches and miniature platforms that they carried with them, drawing crowds to hear about their nostrums or their ability to pull teeth or to grow hair back that had long since fallen out.

Amidst the raised voices came the music of a lute and then of a shawm, being played alternately, each accompanying a pleasant baritone song. Huber wove his way through the crowd to find a small group of people circling a minstrel.

He was a comely young fellow in his early twenties, dressed in a garish red tunic with yellow sleeves. Bareheaded with long blond hair, Hubert could see why more than half of his audience were female. Both instruments had straps looped over his neck so that he could dexterously swap them with barely a gap in the music. By his feet was a drum and another stringed instrument.

Hubert stood and listened as the minstrel went through a medley of ballads and comic songs that he had clearly composed himself. Hubert half expected some to contain snippets of news from other parts of the country, for that was expected of wandering minstrels.

Just then two men and a woman, all young like the minstrel, broke into his circle, causing him to suddenly stop.

'Why, what have we here?' he asked the audience. 'Three worthy people dressed as clowns. What are they, do you good people think?'

'Jongleurs!' cried a young urchin. 'I saw them practising by the pond.'

'They've got painted faces,' called a young girl. 'They're funny.'

And suddenly from inside their clothes, the three drew out brightly coloured wooden clubs and proceeded to juggle, much to the delight of the crowd. As they did the audience moved back, giving them room.

'You are right, young sir!' cried the minstrel as he began to play his lute, slowly at first but gradually picking up pace. And as he played, the trio juggled faster. Then they weaved in and out, tossing the clubs to each other in such an intricate and adroit manner that it was hard for the eye to follow.

'What-ho! Can you do more than that?' queried the minstrel.

'Why aye, we can, Master Minstrel,' said the woman. 'We can tumble.'

Laying their clubs aside, all three proceeded to walk on their hands, then flicked upright once more. There followed a series of somersaults and finally, one man vaulted onto his fellow's shoulders, and then the woman scaled up them both to stand upon the shoulders of the second, so that they formed a human tower.

'Oh dear, they are wobbling!' cried the minstrel as he strummed his lute. 'Take care! Give them room, for they may —'

There was much laughter from the crowd as the tumbler on the bottom teetered this way and that, causing the two above to sway and squeal.

'Tumble!' called out the minstrel, and as if on order they did just that, all three performing a somersault to end up on their feet one in front of the other.

'We thank you, people of Merrie Wakefield,' called out the woman, her painted mouth beaming. 'We are the Barnsdale Tumbling and Jongling Troupe and we bring you a show of magic, dance, music and tumbling. Join us over by the church when you hear our minstrel ring a bell in just a few minutes.'

The audience cheered and laughed, though few spared any coins for the impromptu preview of their show.

'Hubert of Loxley, my friend,' cried out a worthy-looking fellow, whom Hubert knew as one of the town constables in charge of the men of the watch. He was wearing a tunic upon which was the badge of office proclaiming his work, and from his belt hung a thick truncheon. 'How are you returned from Winchester? What news of the Royal Court?'

Hubert had not wanted to tell of the events in Winchester, but now he saw that he had little choice.

'Jack Newson, my old friend. I can tell you that I am pleased to be back in Wakefield.'

'Oh, you can do better than that. Tell me all. Why not share a jug of ale with me at the Golden Fleece Tavern? I could manage a drink after wandering the streets all night with my men of the night watch.'

Hubert gave a short laugh and shook his head. 'I wish that I could take a drink, Jack, but not this day. Sir Richard will be opening the court session at one o'clock and unlike you, I am not excused. I must keep a clear head.'

Jack Newson gave him a dig in the ribs. 'Well then, tell me all right here and now. What gossip from court? Any news about King Edward and his wife, our Queen Philippa? Or Queen Isabella —'

There was a sudden cry and raised voices from behind them. Hubert turned in time to see the minstrel grabbing the female tumbler's blouse and cursing her with the foulest language. The two men remonstrated with him, but he headbutted one in the face and struck the other with his fist, splitting his lip and spraying blood.

'Fight! Fight!' The cry went up and immediately the departing audience and many more started crowding around them.

The tumbler with the split lip recovered and threw himself at the minstrel. They went down to the ground, flailing and kicking and punching at each other. The woman tried to pull the minstrel off the other, but he tossed her aside and sprang to his feet, grabbing two of the juggling clubs in the process.

The two male tumblers charged at him, but one went down with a club on the head and the other was felled when a club connected with his groin.

'Enough!' cried Hubert. 'I am the assistant to Sir Richard Lee and I order you to stop!' He grabbed the minstrel's wrist and wrenched the club from his hand. Constable Newson did likewise with the other, and together they held him firmly.

'He's mad!' cried the woman tumbler. 'He just went mad.'

'Well, fellow, what say you to that?' Hubert demanded.

But the minstrel was not looking at him. He seemed to be staring straight ahead, his eyes glazed. Then foam started to bubble from his mouth and he began to shake violently.

Hubert and Jack let go of his wrists and he fell to the ground, where he proceeded to shake and writhe on the dirt and straw.

'He's having a fit!' exclaimed Hubert.

'What should we do?' asked Jack.

Suddenly an authoritative voice cried out in an Irish accent. 'Stand aside, all of you, and let me through!'

Hubert recognised the impressive figure of the physician Doctor Brandon Flynn approach. He had a long, well-groomed red beard and he was holding his medical satchel against his chest. He was a man of about forty years, dressed in a long red and purple striped robe with a furred hood typical of his profession.

'He may swallow his tongue and die,' the doctor announced as he bent beside the writhing man. He opened his satchel and drew out an ivory spatula such as he used for preparing his powders and potions. Then, prising open the man's lower jaw, he inserted the ivory above the tongue and depressed it.

'I need to hold this steady until the fit subsides,' he said.

The minstrel's eyes were open, but the eyeballs had turned upwards so that only the whites could be seen, while his body bucked and shook. All the while the physician held his ivory spatula in his mouth. After a while the rigors slowly lessened, and finally stopped. His eyes closed.

'He will sleep for a few moments,' Doctor Flynn told Hubert over his shoulder. He removed his spatula and wiped it on his sleeve.

The three tumblers were among the onlookers, one of the men with a bleeding head wound and the other with blood on his tunic from his split lip.

'He needs locking up in the stocks!' said the female tumbler.

Hubert looked at Jack Newson and both nodded.

'He will be taken into custody,' Hubert told the woman. 'Sir Richard Lee will be informed and we will see what he decides.'

The minstrel stirred and blinked rapidly before sitting up and rubbing his eyes. Then his mouth opened wide in shock.

'What? Where? Who are you?' he blurted out to the doctor.

'Look what you did, Rupert Bisley,' the woman said accusingly, pointing to her two fellow tumblers. 'We'll have nothing more to do with you, you … you … madman!'

'You're for the stocks,' said the split-lipped fellow.

'Aye, and we're going to pelt your head with these,' said his comrade, holding up two juggling clubs.

Hubert signalled to Jack and, taking an arm each, they hefted the minstrel up to his feet. 'You are under arrest for brawling and attacking these men.'

'Take care of him,' said Doctor Flynn. 'The man is not well.'

'He'll be watched,' returned Hubert.

Doctor Flynn rose and picked up his satchel. He looked at the injured tumblers. 'You two had better come to my surgery so I can take a look at those wounds.' He turned to Hubert. 'Will he be taken before Sir Richard this afternoon?'

'If Sir Richard agrees.'

'Then I will attend the court myself, for his malady needs to be explained.'

'Aye, and we three will be there to see he gets what he deserves,' said the woman.

The minstrel looked dazed. 'My instruments — I must have them.' Then, still confused, he addressed the woman imploringly. 'Agnes, what happened?'

'You happened, you stupid oaf, and we'll have no more of you. If this Sir Richard has any sense he'll put you in the stocks until you rot. We've had enough of you ruining our shows.'

Hubert and Jack Newson frogmarched the minstrel towards the Moot Hall accompanied by a crowd of curious onlookers, including the female tumbler, her two companions having followed Doctor Flynn to his surgery. She continued to verbally berate the minstrel.

They passed a small group who were clustered around Friar Simon in the Tolbooth square. In the centre stood the currently empty stocks and pillory. As these instruments of public punishment were built on raised ground, it gave him a slight platform from which to preach and beg for alms.

'You'll be in those soon enough, Rupert Bisley,' said the woman.

'That's for Sir Richard to decide,' Hubert told her.

Friar Simon picked up his bowl and ran ahead of them. Turning, he bent and peered into the face of the confused minstrel. The remnants of dried froth were still visible about his mouth.

'This man has the look of one possessed,' he announced. 'I see a demon in his eyes.'

'That friar is right,' the woman called out to the muttering crowd. 'We've long thought it: he's got a demon inside him.'

12

After depositing the minstrel in the cells of the Tolbooth, a squat single-storey stone building with barred windows and a stout iron-studded wooden door, Hubert had gone to the Moot Hall where he knew he would find Sir Richard in the Rolls Office. There he explained to Richard about the fracas at the market and his arrest of the minstrel.

'Doctor Flynn was there, my lord, and he treated the man. He said he could have swallowed his tongue and so he held it down until the fit stopped. He said he will come to the court, because the man was ill.'

'It sounds like the falling sickness,' Richard mused as he sat back in his chair and lay down the list that John of Flanshaw had prepared. The court bailiff was sitting on a stool in attendance on Richard.

'If I may speak, Sir Richard?' he asked. When Richard nodded, he went on, 'I know of no one in Wakefield with such an illness.'

Richard looked at Hubert. 'And you arrested him because he had assaulted these tumbling people?'

'Aye, my lord. The two men were both injured, one with a split lip and the other with a head injury after he was hit with one of the juggling clubs. The woman said that the minstrel's name was Rupert Bisley and that they wanted no more to do with him. She said he'd ruined their shows more than once. I had listened to him before it happened, and he seemed a skilled musician with a fine voice.'

'So he is in the cells in the Tolbooth now?'

'He is, my lord. But there is more to hear. As we were taking him to the cells we passed Friar Simon, and he said that he could see a demon in his eyes.'

'A demon!' exclaimed the bailiff, making the sign of the cross.

Hubert's hand went to touch his arrowhead through his tunic. 'Aye. But there was worse to come. No sooner had we got him in the cells than he fell down and had another fit. Luckily, we had seen how Doctor Flynn had treated him so we opened his mouth and used the key to the cell to hold his tongue down. The fit stopped after a while and we lay him on the cot. Jack Newson is there with him still.'

'These tumblers, where are they?'

'The two men went with Doctor Flynn and the woman is outside the Moot Hall, my lord. She is most eager to see the minstrel charged. I imagine that her fellow performers will return promptly with the doctor.'

Richard considered for a few moments, then turned to John of Flanshaw. 'The court will begin in less than an hour. You had best go and open the court hall and make the preparations, including juror selection. Arrange to have the prisoners who are to be tried today brought from the Tolbooth to the cells here, and then see these tumblers and tell them that they are obliged to speak in court when the case is heard.'

With a bow the bailiff left the office to go through to the court hall to open the great doors to let the people in. After careful consideration he approached twelve men of higher social rank to act as jurors. None dissented or complained, but accepted their duty.

After that he passed on the order to the constables to have the prisoners in the Tolbooth brought to the Moot Hall to await their turn. Having done that he found and talked with the tumbling troupe woman, who appeared to be their spokesperson, and informed her that they all would likely be called to give evidence. He duly returned to the Rolls Office with his usual efficiency.

'The court hall has filled up, Sir Richard. The constables and men of the watch are in attendance and I have appointed twelve jurors, so we are ready whenever you wish to proceed.'

Richard tapped the list with his finger. 'We have three cases of criminal damage, three accused thefts, four guild disputes and a number of financial disagreements, but this minstrel case sounds as if it requires attention straight away. We shall make this the first case.'

The cacophony of almost two hundred voices was quite considerable as John of Flanshaw opened the door from the corridor into the court hall.

The bailiff strode up the steps to the dais and stood in front of the large oak table. He rapped his staff loudly three times on the floor and called out in his booming voice: 'Silence in the court for Sir Richard Lee, Circuit Judge of His Majesty King Edward the Third's Northern Realm and of the Manor of Wakefield.'

Richard entered wearing his iron-grey coif, the close cap that was his badge of office as a Sergeant-at-Law. Several steps behind him walked Hubert. They mounted the dais, where Richard took his seat behind the table and Hubert stood behind him and a little to his right.

Richard sat for a few moments, surveying the sight before him. There were no chairs or stools in the main body of the hall since all except the officials were expected to stand in attendance. A three-sided wooden pen faced the table for whoever was addressing the court or being addressed by the judge. To the left of the dais there was a line of twelve stools for the twelve selected members of the jury, who would consider any criminal case that Richard instructed them to decide upon.

The hall was packed as usual. Burghers, guildsmen, tradesmen, yeomen, bondsmen and villains were all standing expectantly. The twelve men that John of Flanshaw had appointed as jurors also stood in front of their stools, and the four constables and their men of the watch stood in a line in front of the dais.

He noted with approval that the tall figure of Doctor Flynn was weaving his way through the crowd to the front, everyone recognising him and giving him leave to pass through.

Richard rapped his gavel on the table. Then he cleared his throat and launched into his usual preamble, in which he lay down the procedure that would be followed in his court.

'People of the Manor of Wakefield and all others who have business with this Manor Court, know you all that I am Sir Richard Lee, Sergeant-at-Law and Circuit Judge of the Northern Realm. It is my duty to demonstrate the fairness of English law to everyone. The jury system that you will see here today is the bastion of our great legal system, and in a few moments these twelve jurors will be sworn in. Their role will be in cases that I decide need an opinion, most essentially in criminal cases. They will hear and in those instances will come to a decision to help me judge. All judgements will be carefully considered and given according to precedent of law. No person should be afraid of the law if they are innocent, but if guilty, then they can expect the appropriate sentence and punishment.'

As he said this, Richard felt a shiver run down his spine.

If only there had been such justice given to the Earl of Kent at his trial in Winchester.

He looked around the court hall at the expectant faces of all present, seeing some worried, others angry or determined as he continued to speak.

'Master John of Flanshaw, the bailiff, will record the events of this court in the Manor Court Rolls.' He pointed to the bailiff's stool at the end of the table where his inkpot, quills and vellum scrolls were laid out in readiness.

'Before we call the first case, the twelve jurors will be sworn in by the bailiff.'

John of Flanshaw approached the table, laid his staff against it and picked up a large Bible before climbing down the steps to swear in each juror in turn.

Once this was completed, Richard rapped his gavel again. 'The Manor Court is now in session. Master John of Flanshaw has given me a list of cases, which will all be duly heard. However, a case has come in that was not on that list but which is of some urgency, so it shall be dealt with first. Bring in Rupert Bisley.'

One of the constables and one of the town watch left the hall and returned a few moments later with the minstrel, whom they escorted in chains to the wooden pen.

'What is your name?' Richard asked.

The minstrel looked dazed, as if he was not yet fully conscious, but he stared up at Richard and blinked before replying, 'I am Rupert Bisley, sir.'

'And you are a minstrel?'

'I am, sir. I'm part of the Barnsdale Tumbling and Jongling Troupe.'

A woman's voice called out, 'Not anymore, he isn't.'

Richard rapped his gavel. 'There will be no crying out in this court unless I ask a question of anyone. That person who did cry out can come forward to the constables, for she will be called to give her testimony when I have finished questioning this prisoner.'

He looked back at the minstrel. 'Rupert Bisley, you have been charged with serious assault upon two members of this tumbling troupe and also of simple assault on a third. How do you plead?'

Rupert Bisley shook his head. 'I am not guilty, sir. I don't know anything about an assault.' He looked at the woman who had come forward to stand with the constables. 'Agnes, you can tell him. I … I cannot remember anything.'

Richard scrutinised the minstrel for a moment, then turned to the jurors. 'I have been informed that this man, purportedly a member of this Barnsdale Tumbling and Jongling Troupe, was playing his instruments in the market and was joined by the rest of the tumbling troupe. It seems that his task was to attract an audience. But, soon after, in an unprovoked attack he assaulted a female member then seriously attacked two men, both of whom I believe have been treated for wounds by Doctor Brandon Flynn. And then, when he was prevented from doing further harm by my assistant Hubert of Loxley here, he fell down and had a fit of some sort.'

He looked at the woman called Agnes. 'Come forward and swear on the Bible that you will tell the truth.'

John of Flanshaw came down from his stool on the dais and held the Bible out to her. She swore to tell the truth.

'Identify yourself,' Richard instructed.

'I am Agnes Moorhead, of the Barnsdale Tumbling and Jongling Troupe. The other members are my husband, Ham

Moorhead, and my brother, Basil Potman. That man Rupert Bisley only joined us a week ago.'

'And was he a good member of your troupe?'

She shrugged her shoulders. 'He's a fair strummer and he has a decent voice, but that's all. He's no tumbler or jongleur. We thought he'd help drum up folk to watch us. But he's messed up a show twice before.'

'By attacking anyone?'

'No, by having one of those attacks of his. It puts people off, him shaking and frothing at the mouth like that. They don't stay, so we don't make any money.'

Richard called the other two tumblers forward and asked a few questions to confirm that they had been attacked without any provocation or warning that day.

Richard saw Doctor Flynn raise his hand.

'Doctor Flynn, you have some part in this. Please step forward, swear on the Bible, and then tell us what you saw.'

The tall physician came forward and swore on the Bible before turning to face Richard. He spoke authoritatively. 'I came across the scene in the market as I was making my way to my surgery. Your assistant, Hubert of Loxley, and one of the constables was standing over the man who is standing in the box. He was having a seizure and was frothing saliva. He looked to be choking and I intervened to prevent him from swallowing his tongue and cutting off his windpipe. He would most assuredly have died if I had not done so.'

'And what is your diagnosis, Doctor Flynn?'

'This man is ill. He has the falling sickness. It explains all that we have heard about the assaults.'

'How so, Doctor Flynn?'

'It is a condition caused by total disruption of the normal balance of the humours, the vital fluids that run through the body.'

'There are four of these, is that not so, Doctor?' Richard said for the benefit of the jurors.

'Indeed, these humours are called blood, black bile, yellow bile and phlegm. Too much of one humour in a part of the body can cause the organs within it to malfunction. For example, too much phlegm in the lungs causes strangulation inside, and the person will cough and struggle to breathe. With the falling sickness, there is too much blood in the head and—'

There was a sudden noise from the wooden pen, and all eyes shifted to see the minstrel's face contort and his eyes bulge. He grasped the railing and his knuckles turned white as his body started to shake violently. Then he collapsed and the sound of thrashing and the kicking of wood filled the court hall.

'Take him out of there at once!' Doctor Flynn commanded. 'Bring him to the front where he can breathe, and then stand aside.'

As a constable and two of the men of the watch carried him and laid him in front of the physician, Doctor Flynn opened his satchel and took out an ivory spatula. People tried to crowd in to see what was happening, but Richard rapped his gavel hard.

'Order in the court! Let the doctor do his work.'

Hubert leaped down from the dais and ordered the constables and men of the watch to keep the onlookers back.

Doctor Flynn repeated the treatment he had given before by prising open the minstrel's lower jaw and inserting the spatula above his tongue to keep it down. Gradually the seizure settled until Rufus Bisley lay at the front of the court, seeming to have fallen into sleep.

'As I was telling you,' the physician went on, 'this man is ill. He has too much blood in his brain and it is worsened by too much phlegm that is affecting his breathing and, as you can see, he foams at the mouth with that excess phlegm.'

'And how does this explain his assaults on the other members of his tumbling troupe?'

'His brain would have been full of blood and phlegm, so that he would have not known what he was doing. He would just have become instantly angered, and he struck out at those who were close to him at the time. Afterwards he would have no memory of it as his humours gradually started to rebalance.' He pointed to the prostrate figure. 'Falling into a deep sleep like this afterwards is quite typical.'

'And what treatment does he need?'

'He needs venesection; that is, he needs to be bled regularly. And he needs special medication that I could compound, made from mugwort, castoreum and possibly *oleum cerebri humani*.'

Richard frowned. He appreciated that only a few folk in the court would know Latin, which he thought was just as well.

'It is a powerful medicine, Sir Richard. If that fails, then he will need trephination: I would bore a hole in his skull to let excess brain blood out.'

Someone started clapping their hands to attract attention, and Richard turned to see Friar Simon in the middle of the crowd. He was gesticulating at Richard.

'Well, Friar Simon, what have you to say?'

'This man is not ill-humoured, Sir Richard. He has *morbus daemonicus* — he is possessed of a demon. I have seen it in his eyes.'

There was a collective intake of breath from the crowd and then much muttering.

Rupert Bisley started to stir. He stretched his arms out, then sat up, yawning and working his jaw from side to side. Putting his fingers to his mouth, he winced as he touched his tongue. He quickly withdrew them and saw they were smeared with blood from a laceration on his tongue. He suddenly appeared startled by so many faces staring down at him and made to stand, but he was pulled to his feet by two of the constables.

'Shall we put him back in the pen, my lord?' one asked.

'Do so. We have not finished yet, for we have yet to consider the assaults on his fellow members of the tumbling troupe.'

Turning to Friar Simon, Richard asked, 'And what do you propose, Friar Simon?'

'He needs to be taken to a holy site to have the demon exorcised.'

'And where would you suggest?'

Doctor Flynn turned and held his hands out beseechingly. 'Sir Richard, surely you do not believe this nonsense? The man is ill; he needs medicine and perhaps a surgical opening of his head.'

'He needs exorcism, holy water, and the presence of a holy relic,' Friar Simon persisted.

'And where might such be found?' Richard asked.

'There are priories and monasteries in Pontefract, Sir Richard, but the closest is Cawthorne Priory in the direction of Barnsdale woods and the road towards Barnsley, beyond the village of Cawthorne. It is of the Gilbertine Order and there is a relic of Saint Gilbert there, as well as an anchoress with a reputation as a great healer.'

'That is most interesting. Would they be willing to take the prisoner and see to him — exorcise this demon if necessary, or use this relic you speak of? Or perhaps this anchoress —'

'She is called Sister Odelina, my lord.'

'Perhaps Sister Odelina could heal him?'

Friar Simon nodded emphatically. 'They never turn away the sick, my lord. They have an infirmary.'

Richard turned to the jurors. 'You have all heard the witnesses and you have actually seen this man have a seizure here in this court. It is, I understand, the third he has had in a short time. The only thing I wish you to consider is whether he is guilty of a premeditated assault on Agnes and Ham Moorhead and upon Basil Potman. If you decide it was the result of some disease or disorder, consider whether it is caused by his humours or possession.'

It took but a few moments of conferring before the spokesman stood and told Richard that they thought he was ill or possessed and had not been in control of himself.

'I agree. Strike off his chains,' Richard said.

The tumblers all mumbled and shook their heads as their former troupe member had his chains removed.

'In which case, I must make my judgement as to how best to deal with this case.' Richard thought for a moment before turning to John of Flanshaw. 'Master John, write a letter to the prior of Cawthorne Priory and inform him that after consideration of this case, and you can describe it as we have heard it, it is the wish of this court that they should kindly do what they can for this man, Rupert Bisley.'

At the mention of his name the minstrel turned and shook his head, as if trying to clear it and rouse himself from a dream.

'My musical instruments, sir?' he asked. 'Can I have my instruments? They are most precious to me.'

'They will go with you,' Richard said, before turning back to the bailiff. 'Tell the prior that Doctor Flynn in Wakefield will make up some medicine for him and he should be informed of his progress.' He turned to the physician. 'Does this sound agreeable to you, Doctor Flynn?'

'It does, Sir Richard, but I fear that I will still need to perform a trephination to open his head.'

'To o-open my head?' the minstrel stuttered.

'If it is needed,' Richard said.

'Then, sir, I pray that it will not be needed,' Bisley said.

'Once I have signed this letter and my seal is attached, have it sent with a messenger,' Richard instructed. 'Meanwhile, the prisoner will remain in the Tolbooth under careful observation. And to begin, Doctor Flynn can make up some of his mugwort or castoreum.'

As Rupert Bisley was led away, Richard signalled for Doctor Flynn to ascend the dais.

'This medicine, *oleum cerebri humani*, means oil of human brain, does it not?' he said softly so none would hear.

'It does, Sir Richard. It is made from the brain of a man who has died a violent death. It is macerated and mixed with salt, then distilled to produce the oil, which is then given with wine. I have used it on occasion with some success, although the pharmacopoeia recommends that it be given in a goblet made from a human skull, again preferably from one who suffered a violent death.'

'This is what I thought, Doctor. Still, I think we should give the priory the opportunity to heal him. It would be less radical than opening his head.' He nodded. 'I thank you for your learned input. If you would now go and make up the medicines, I would be grateful.'

John of Flanshaw had deftly written the letter to the priory, which he presented to Richard to sign, and then make his seal.

Once done, Richard rapped his gavel.

'And now, the next case.'

13

Cawthorne Priory

Two days later Hubert was given the task of riding to Cawthorne to deliver Rupert Bisley into the care of Prior Dominic at Cawthorne Priory. Hubert led the way on the ten-mile journey, riding his horse, while the minstrel had been given a donkey. Beside them, walking steadily with a stout staff, was Friar Simon, who had been only too happy when Richard asked him to accompany them to the priory. He had declined the offer of a donkey, replying that his maker had furnished him with two good legs.

Over the two days that the minstrel had spent in the Tolbooth cell, he had only had one further seizure, which was attributed to the efficacy of the medicine that Doctor Flynn had compounded. Both Hubert and Friar Simon had visited him several times, and on each occasion Rupert was in good spirits, demonstrated by the fact that he was contentedly playing either his lute or his shawm and singing either traditional songs or ones that he had just composed.

He had entertained the other prisoners, of whom there were six, and their jailors. Hubert thought him to be a merry fellow.

'So, do you think these religious brothers and sisters will cure me of my malady, Hubert?' Rupert asked as they wended their way through Barnsdale Forest.

'I hope so, Rupert.'

Friar Simon was less reticent. 'I am sure that they will be able to drive the demon from you, my son.'

Rupert pursed his lips. 'If it is truly a demon, Friar. I am not so sure, because I have had this horrible affliction since I was a child.' He gave a shrug of resignation. 'Yet I have managed to live as well as I can. Music and song help, which is why I have chosen the life I have as a wandering minstrel.'

Friar Simon laughed. 'There is much to be said for wandering, my son. I was a soldier when I was but a lad and fought in many a battle, just as good Hubert of Loxley here has done.'

'As has my master, Sir Richard Lee,' interjected Hubert. 'He took an arrow in his leg at Boroughbridge in 1322. He was a sergeant-at-law already, but it was after the battle that King Edward the Second made him the judge of this Northern Realm.'

'Then I like Sir Richard even more,' said Rupert. 'He showed me kindness, rather than tossing me in prison or putting me in the stocks or pillory to be pelted with dung or stones until I had another fit or died.'

'Sir Richard is a wise judge,' Friar Simon agreed with a nod.

'But that doctor did not think I have a demon — he wanted to open my head.'

Hubert clicked his tongue. 'Doctor Flynn is a good doctor, whom Sir Richard holds in high esteem. I also know that he is greatly skilled. If those at the priory are not successful, then he may still have to open your head.'

'He will not need to, of that I am sure,' said the friar. 'As sure as I was when the Lord spoke to me and told me to turn from my brawling ways, which I have to say I was good at. I was never defeated.'

Hubert looked down from his horse at Friar Simon and smiled. 'Yet you did sustain a few knocks and broken noses in your time.'

'That I did, Hubert. And I know that you are wondering how you would have fared against me, man to man.' Before Hubert could answer, he laughed and went on, 'But that neither of us will ever know, for I am a man of peace now and preach only good Christian charity.'

'Well said, Friar Simon,' said Hubert, a little relieved. Then, changing the subject, he asked the minstrel, 'Will you miss performing with the tumbling troupe, Rupert?'

'I will, but I hope that I may either find them again, or join another group when I am cured.'

'But you are not a tumbler yourself?' Friar Simon asked.

'No, but I can do other types of jongling. I can make things appear and vanish.' He opened the purse that hung from his belt and pulled out a copper coin. He tossed it into the air with one hand and, reaching up with the other, caught it. He held up his closed fist. 'Like this!' He opened his hand to reveal that it was empty.

Both Hubert and Friar Simon laughed.

'A clever trick, Rupert,' said the friar.

'It is no great trick; I use a coin that can change itself into a fly that is so small you cannot see it.' He made a show of looking hither and thither and suddenly snatched at the air. This time, when he opened the closed fist they saw a silver coin resting on his palm.

'Sometimes he is a tricky fly and changes into a more valuable coin, like that. Or —' He tossed it again and caught it in the other hand, only to reveal upon opening his palm that it had changed yet again into a small brass key. 'Or into my treasure box key.'

He made to toss it into the air again, but it had once again vanished.

'There it is,' he said, his eyes moving as if following an invisible object arcing in the air to land with a clinking sound in his purse. 'It flies back there to the safety of my purse.'

Friar Simon slapped Rupert on the back. 'A magical skill, Rupert. And where is this treasure box of yours?'

'It follows us, flying through the air like an invisible fairy.'

'A good fairy or a bad fairy?' Friar Simon asked.

'Oh, a good one. It is just a pity that it can't overcome this demon that you say is inside me.'

'Then perhaps it is not an entirely good fairy,' said Friar Simon. 'Perhaps it is as changeable as this mystical coin and key of yours?'

Hubert noted a flash of fear crossing Rupert's face. Then it was gone.

Without thinking, his hand went to touch his arrowhead through his tunic.

They passed through Deffer Forest and then followed a babbling brook that cut through ridge and furrows and larger pastures with herds of sheep and cattle to rise to the hamlet of Cawthorne with its village green and tavern. As they rode, Rupert took out his lute and started to sing. They therefore accumulated a gaggle of urchins, who trotted beside them until they dropped down again into a valley and yet more woodland, before starting a slow ascent towards the imposing buildings of Cawthorne Priory atop a hill.

'This is most unusual, is it not? Nuns and monks living together,' Rupert said.

Friar Simon shook his head. 'They worship in the same community and the same church, but the priory really consists of a church and a nunnery and a monastery. They do not actually ever meet, even when they are in the church at the same time.'

'How so?' asked Rupert.

'As you will see when we arrive, the church is the central building. The nunnery's cloister is built onto the northern transept and the chapter house, kitchens, refectory and all the other buildings lead off it. The monks' monastery is virtually a mirror image of it, but it is separate to the east of the church. The two are linked by a long corridor passage that halfway along opens out into a window house.'

'Is this so they can look through and see each other?' Hubert asked.

Friar Simon laughed. 'No, even there the monks and nuns cannot see each other. It is called this not because it has actual windows, but because it contains a large *fenestra versatilis*. That is Latin and means versatile or changeable window.'

Rupert laughed. 'I am no wiser.'

'It isn't a window at all, but a large turntable that has several sections. The nuns, who do all the cooking for the monks, transfer the food by putting it in one section, and as they turn it the monks take it out from their side.'

'And do the monks do all the manual work for the nuns in exchange?'

Again Friar Simon laughed. 'No, because you see there are not just nuns and monks. The priory actually consists of four communities — you'll recognise them by the clothes they wear. The nuns wear a black tunic and matching habit, with a white scapular round their shoulders. They also wear a white lamb's wool headdress with a coarse cotton veil. The lay sisters, who assist the nuns, wear a black tunic without a scapular. They have a sheepskin cloak and a long hood, but without the veil worn by the nuns.

'The monks wear a black cassock with a white hooded cloak and usually red leather shoes. The lay brothers who assist them wear a dark tunic and rough skin cloak.'

'How many nuns and monks are there?' Hubert ventured.

'Prior Dominic is in charge of the monastery and the whole priory. Mother Griselda is the Mother Superior of the nunnery. There are about fourteen monks and about thirty or so lay brothers. Under Mother Griselda there are about twenty nuns and forty or so lay sisters.'

Hubert waved his hand at the surrounding lands with their livestock and neatly tended fields. 'So who does all this work?'

'The nunnery and the monastery have separate farms. The lay brothers and the lay sisters do all the farm work and the manual work so that the nuns and monks can devote themselves to the spiritual functions of the priory.'

As they left the woods and approached the priory, they saw that it was surrounded by a high sandstone wall. A lay brother stood outside a gatehouse watching their approach, and as they made the final ascent he waved in greeting and then pulled a rope that rang a bell in a small belfry above the gatehouse. The gates were opened from the inside and they entered an outer cobbled courtyard. Two monks were awaiting them in front of a set of steps leading up to a great door. One was tall and the other at least a foot shorter and quite portly. Both had their hands together but hidden under the sleeves of their black habits.

As Hubert and Rupert dismounted, two lay brothers hurried forth to take their reins.

'My friends, welcome to Cawthorne Priory,' said the taller monk with a big smile as he led the way across the cobbles in his red leather shoes to greet them. 'I am Prior Dominic, and this is Father Robert, the hospitaller.'

They all exchanged bows as Friar Simon introduced them in turn.

'Prior Dominic, I thank you for taking me in,' said Rupert. 'And if you can cure me of this malady, I shall be eternally grateful.'

Prior Dominic smiled. 'It is the Lord's work to help where and whenever we can. Sir Richard Lee explained everything to me in his letter. If there is indeed a demon inside you, then Father Robert here will be involved in dealing with it.'

'And if there is no demon, I can perhaps give you physic that will help,' said the portly monk. 'But before we do anything at all, I would like to just watch you for a day or two in the hospital.'

Prior Dominic reached out a hand and patted Friar Simon's arm. 'And our good friend, will you be staying to watch as well?'

Friar Simon cupped his hands together, blew into them, and then rubbed them together vigorously. 'If that is possible, Prior Dominic, I would appreciate it. It may be the age of these old bones of mine, but I feel the cold more these days.'

'You are most welcome to stay in the guest house of the monastery,' said Prior Dominic, turning and holding out his hand towards the steps. 'I shall lead the way to the calefactory where you can get warm and slake your thirst, and then we shall show you all around the priory before we sup.'

'The calefactory is the warming room,' Friar Simon explained as they followed the two monks. 'It is the only place in the monastery where a fire is permitted. The nunnery also has one, but in addition they also have heat in the kitchen and the laundry.'

Hubert nodded grudging acceptance. Sir Richard had warned him that although the inhabitants of the priory enjoyed living in rather spacious and grand surroundings, they had limited creature comforts like heat, food and entertainment.

The monastery was, as Friar Simon had intimated on the journey, a mirror image of the nunnery, except that the nunnery cloister was built onto the transept wall of the church. The living quarters for the monks consisted of individual cells, and the dormitories for the lay brothers were all reached by stairs from the covered arcade of the cloister that surrounded the square court. The chapter house where the monks and lay brothers attended meetings was a large square building on the south-east corner of the cloister and was the second most impressive building in the complex after the church itself. The library and scriptorium was also large and had about twenty cubicles, many of which were currently in use by monks who were writing or illustrating parchment or vellums. The hospital was a long L-shaped building separated from the monastery, as was usual in order to keep the ill away from the healthy.

Then there were the buildings concerned with the material needs of the community: the brewhouse, the bakery, the buttery, a lime kiln and a farrier and blacksmith's yard, which were also set apart so that the spiritual and physical aspects of the life of the community were kept separate.

In all of the buildings they were shown by Prior Dominic they saw monks and lay brothers hard at work.

'It is like a whole town,' commented Hubert. 'There is lots of noise — hammering, sawing, tapping and so forth, and yet it is strangely quiet.'

'There is no singing, jesting, laughing or whistling,' murmured Rupert.

'And no talking,' added Friar Simon in a whisper.

'It is not a strict rule of our Order, but by choice we restrict speech except during worship, when eating, or when visiting the reredorter,' explained Prior Dominic. 'I will introduce you to some of our monks, but do not expect much conversation.'

'Talking is permitted in the hospital, of course,' added Father Robert, 'for many of the patients who come to us are not from the monastery. This you will find out when I show you the hospital, Master Rupert.'

Later, as they entered the refectory, the hum of voices and occasional soft laughter were quite startling in comparison with the quiet in the cloister and the rest of the monastery.

Prior Dominic invited Hubert, Rupert and Simon to sit at the high table in front of the altar while they waited for the rest of the monks and lay brothers to file in and take their places at either the high table or the three long tables that ran the length of the refectory. Prior Dominic and Father Robert sat in the middle of the high table and introduced them to the other senior monks sitting with them.

'Father Joseph is our librarian,' the prior said, indicating an elderly monk with copious silver hair circling his tonsure. 'He knows many languages and has probably read every book in our possession.'

'We have books and scrolls in English, Latin, Greek and Hebrew,' the elderly monk said enthusiastically. 'If Prior Dominic allows it, I can show you some of our most treasured Bibles. And if you are interested, I can show you my mapping of the stars and my own rather inadequate work on astronomy. We have in the library a copy of *De Dracone* by Walcher of Lorraine, who was the prior of Malvern two centuries ago. The things he could calculate with his astrolabe were years ahead—'

Prior Dominic could see that the librarian was about to go into an impromptu lecture so gave permission, adding, 'If our guests are here long enough, Father Joseph.'

'And I would be happy to show them the scriptorium, Prior Dominic,' said a middle-aged monk, who screwed his eyes up as he scrutinised the guests.

'Father Christopher is in charge of our scriptorium, and also supervises the nuns' illumination work. He is an artist and looks after all of the inks, vellums and parchment that are used in the preparation of our manuscripts.'

The monk smiled and held up a magnifying glass that hung from a leather cord about his neck. 'Unfortunately, the many years that I have spent with all this fine writing has worn my eyes out, and I now bless this wonderful glass that helps me to see and continue my work.' He pointed it down towards the middle table and appeared to be looking affectionately at someone seated in the midst of the young faces. 'Fortunately, there are many with younger eyes who will be able to follow me and carry on with my work.'

Prior Dominic patted his arm. 'But you will be able to carry on for many years, Father Christopher, have no fear.' He then indicated an unsmiling monk at the end of the table. 'Father Barnabas is our choirmaster.'

Rupert brightened. 'Ah, a musician, like myself. Perhaps we could sing together?'

He was greeted with a less than enthusiastic response. 'You are welcome to sing in our services,' the surly monk replied, then turned to look down at his clasped hands.

Prior Dominic whispered, 'Father Barnabas has a strong opinion that the singing voice is only for God's ears in church.'

Rupert looked crestfallen. 'Does that mean that I may not play my instruments?'

Prior Dominic smiled kindly. 'Our rules do not apply to our guests or visiting pilgrims. You are at liberty to play in our cloister and also in the chapter house or the calefactory. I am sure that the monks and brothers will enjoy your music.'

'Are all of the lay brothers here to become monks?' Hubert asked.

Prior Dominic smiled. 'No, the vast majority of lay brothers are quite content to live and work here in God's presence. As you can see, many are just boys, as young as ten. When they reach the age of fifteen, they can request to join the Order of Saint Gilbert. We monks follow the Augustinian rule, and our nuns take the Benedictine rule.'

He pointed to two monks who had just entered and taken seats at the high table.

'Father Matthew is our Novice Master,' he said, introducing the guests to the first, a tall, almost skeletally thin man with a wispy fringe of ginger hair around his tonsure. 'He accepts suitably devout brothers to become postulants to be trained and instructed until they are twenty years of age. Then, if we are all agreed, they become novitiates.'

'Indeed,' said Father Matthew, pointing to his bald pate with its ring of ginger hair. 'At that point they take holy orders, receive a new name and for the first time have a tonsure.'

'And after two years as a novice, if all of the monks agree, he can become a full canon, like us. Then he may take services and hear the confessions of monks, brothers, nuns and lay sisters.'

'And is it the same length of time and training for nuns?' Hubert asked.

'No,' replied Father Matthew. 'A girl may become a lay sister at twelve and take the Rule of Benedict at sixteen and become a nun. But in that time they study in Greek and Latin and receive spiritual guidance and instruction.'

Prior Dominic pointed down the long tables. 'You can see some of our novices, part of whose purpose is to supervise and instruct the lay brothers. There at the middle table is Father Luke, one of our newest canons. He instructs the novitiates in psalms just as he was instructed by Father Matthew. And he also has the task of seeing to the physical and spiritual needs of the distinguished guests in the hospitium.'

Hubert saw a youthful-looking monk with black hair and tonsure, smiling and jesting with two younger novitiates and with lay brothers further down the table.

The prior introduced the other monk who had sat down at the high table. 'And this is Father Jacob, our most necessary administrator and treasurer, who oversees the finances of the priory.'

Hubert thought that the monk looked more like a brewer master, for his nose was covered in red veins like many a heavy drinker he had known.

Everyone sat in silence while Prior Dominic stood at a lectern and read out a passage from the Bible before saying grace. Then several lay brothers came from the refectory passageway that was connected to the nunnery by the window house that Simon had told them about, bearing trays of steaming hot food. They went along both sides of the table, efficiently distributing bowls, portions of vegetable stew and hunks of bread. At the same time more brothers passed along, pouring ale into each person's mug.

'Will it be possible to visit the nunnery?' Hubert asked the prior as he tried to hide his disappointment at the meagre ration he had been given. 'Sir Richard Lee, my master, was most eager that I should convey his good wishes to the Mother Superior. As I believe he mentioned in his letter, he asked whether a relic of a saint could help Rupert, or that the anchoress could heal him.'

Prior Dominic nodded. 'Indeed. Tomorrow I shall take you to the nun's half of the community and show you the church and, if Mother Griselda is willing, perhaps even see the anchoress's cell in the church.'

'If her cell is inside the church, is she able to come out and walk within the church, worship with the other nuns?' Hubert asked.

'No, there is no door. Sister Odelina's cell is behind the altar, and she has been sealed inside.'

Rupert shook his head in disbelief. 'I must say that I cannot imagine how anyone could possibly survive by detaching themselves from the rest of the world.'

Prior Dominic smiled. 'But she has not. She can still see the sky and she can see the high altar in the church and the nuns during a service. Most importantly, she has given herself entirely to the Lord.'

'It is not so different to yourself,' said Hubert. 'You all live in an enclosed community. You do not have the freedom that Friar Simon has, for example. He can come and go as he pleases and visit wherever and whoever he wants.'

'And find out what is happening in the world,' Simon said as he finished his mug of ale. 'But here you don't really know what evil is happening in the country.'

'Do you refer to the execution of Edmund of Woodstock, the Earl of Kent?'

'Why, yes, as a matter of fact — that is just what I meant,' Simon replied. 'It is news that I only heard myself a few days ago, when Hubert of Loxley and Sir Richard Lee returned to Wakefield. How did you hear of this?'

Hubert was aware that much of the chatter around them had ceased.

'We are not so enclosed as you think, Friar Simon,' replied Prior Dominic. 'We often send monks or brothers to other priories of our order or to monasteries and nunneries of other orders, such as the Dominicans or Cluniacs. Or to the great cities, if there are messages or letters that we need to have delivered to archbishops, bishops, administrators or judges like Sir Richard. Two of our monks have in fact recently returned from such journeys and had collected news along the way.' He pointed along the table. 'Father Matthew is one who has recently returned from such a mission.'

Father Matthew nodded but continued to devote his attention to his food.

'And we also have many pilgrims who visit us and stay in the undercrofts for several days, or as long as they wish. Even today we have had two arrive not long after yourselves, wishing to see the birth girdle of Sister Odelina and the relic of Saint Gilbert.'

'Are they seated here?' Hubert asked, glancing around.

'No, they will eat with the other pilgrims. There are about eight or so at any time. Father Robert has to ensure that they do not have leprosy or the pox in the first instance. Just as he has to examine every person who comes to us — apart, of course, from distinguished guests, or special representatives such as yourself.'

'Or old friends like me,' added Friar Simon.

'And do they pay you to stay here?' Rupert asked.

'No, but they may make a donation if they wish.'

'And of course they will bring news that they have heard along the way,' added Simon.

Prior Dominic nodded. 'And we also have accommodation — the guest house in the nunnery and the hospitium in the monastery for distinguished guests who come to consult Sister Odelina or to be healed with the birth girdle or the relic of Saint Gilbert.'

'Have you any distinguished guests staying at the moment?' Hubert asked.

Prior Dominic shook his head. 'No, but we are expecting some tonight.'

Hubert was not sure, but he thought he saw a flicker of fear cross the prior's face.

14

There were several places in the nunnery where they kept their secret assignations and where, when opportunity permitted, they made love.

'Are we truly wicked?' the young sister asked as they parted, reluctantly putting on their habits.

'It is normal and natural, Sister.'

'But we have both given ourselves to —'

'To each other.'

The young sister giggled. 'I didn't mean that. I meant —'

'I know exactly what you meant and I am just teasing you.'

'But will we be damned for enjoying the pleasures of the flesh?'

'Why should we be? We are not the only ones. I told you before — there are older, more senior ones than us who have done much worse.'

'Do you mean —?'

'As I said, much worse.'

'I can't help but feel guilty when I see everyone else at prayer, knowing that we have…'

'Many so-called sins are being committed on both sides of the priory. We love each other, so it cannot be wrong.'

They kissed again, passionately.

'We just have to ensure that we are never caught.'

There were some twenty patients currently in the monastery hospital. About half were lay brothers and the other half an assortment of villagers, yeomen, serfs and vagabonds.

'We have people suffering from all types of malady here,' Father Robert explained to Rupert that evening as he showed him to his bed in the hospital's open dormitory.

Rupert nodded as he listened to the cacophony of snatched conversations interspersed with moans of pain, the occasional shriek of agony, and the peppering of coughs and other bodily noises.

'So what do you need to do?' Rupert asked as he handed him the chamber pot that the hospitaller had asked him to fill with urine. 'Do you want to look at my head, in my mouth or into my eyes?'

'I shall look at all three in due course, but first of all I must look at your water.'

From a pouch hanging from his waist cord, Father Robert took out a round-bottomed glass flask with a thin neck. Into this he poured a quantity of urine from the chamber pot.

'I am a fully trained physician as well as a monk,' he explained as he swirled the urine around in the flask. 'This is a matula, which enables me to tell much about your body.'

From the pouch he took out a tile on which a wheel was depicted. Around it were small circles, each filled with a different colour, from white all the way round to red.

'By comparing the colour of your urine with this wheel I can tell if you have any of these twenty diseases, each of which indicates an imbalance in your humours. Those are the vital fluids that run through the organs of your body.'

'Doctor Flynn said he thought I had too much blood in my head. That is what he said caused my attacks.'

Father Robert held the matula up to the candle that guttered in the sconce on the wall. Then he slowly shook his head.

'I cannot see that at the moment. This urine is clear.'

'Does that mean that I do not have too much blood in my head?'

'It doesn't look like it — at this moment! But it might show if you were about to have or had just had an attack. The humours can pass through you like babbling streams or raging torrents.'

'I am told that it is as if a rage flows through me and bursts out in a flood of violence.'

The physician gestured for Rupert to sit upon the cot and, taking his head in both hands, he leaned close to look into first one eye and then the other.

'No, I cannot see anything other than your pupils, and all they show me are mirror images of myself.'

'Yourself? I do not understand.'

The monk laughed. 'Then look into mine and you will see a reflection of yourself in each of my eyes.'

Rupert did so and then gave a short laugh. 'A remarkable thing! The black pupil is like a tiny mirror.'

'And that it is how the pupil received its name. It is from the Latin *pupilla*, which means small doll. The Roman physicians first called it thus, because it showed an image like a small doll.'

'So, if you cannot see anything in my eyes and my urine shows nothing to be wrong, does that mean that there is no demon in me?' Rupert asked hopefully.

Father Robert put a hand on the minstrel's shoulder then made the sign of the cross in the air before him. 'It is not as simple as that, I am afraid. Since nothing shows in your urine, it makes it more likely that you do indeed have a demon inside you. A sleeping demon that is not showing itself at this time.'

Lanterns had been lit around the monks' cloister that evening. Rupert and Hubert strolled around it, both well wrapped against the cold but enjoying the moonlight that tried to break through the cloudy sky. Rupert had his lute and when they reached the northeastern corner of the cloister, they sat and he began to strum.

'I'm glad that Prior Dominic said that I could play, for I must admit to being worried about whatever they plan to do to me. Father Robert said that there may be a demon inside me and that he may just be sleeping at the moment. Music and song will mayhap calm me and keep the demon asleep.' He began to play and sing.

Hubert admired the skill with which his fingers moved and wished that he had learned to play an instrument.

Rupert sang one ballad after another, his voice carrying on the night air.

Throughout the priory, monks, nuns, sisters and brothers heard his song and momentarily stopped whatever they were doing to listen.

Many were entranced.

Some were moved to tears.

One was angered.

And another smiled as they saw opportunity.

Sister Odelina was in a deep, troubled sleep. She had felt unsettled since her angel had spoken to her, and she had prayed until exhaustion had forced her to lie on her cot. Night came, and then she heard the comforting sound of Matins at two bells, before drifting off to sleep once more.

'Odelina! Odelina! Awake.'

She gasped and sat up on her cot. 'I am here.'

'You must beware the evil. You cannot trust anyone.'

'Not even Mother Griselda?'

'No one.'

'Or Prior Dominic?'

'No one. Witchcraft and Dark Arts are being practised in this consecrated place.'

'But … but by whom?'

'Trust no one. Beware, Odelina. If you talk to anyone — anyone at all — even those you trust, tell them nothing.'

'But Mother S—'

'Tell them nothing!' the voice hissed. 'There is treachery everywhere. Even here.'

It was between Matins and Lauds of the Dead. They lay naked on the cot, not feeling the cold after the heat and intensity of their lovemaking.

'I cannot stay long or my brothers will miss me in the dormitory.'

'Stay a while longer. You brighten up this cell of mine when we lie together, and you make me feel as if the years have fallen from me like the leaves fall in autumn. I live for your company and your touch.'

'Even though we commit mortal sins each time we meet and risk the fires of Hell?'

'I would gladly walk through the fiery gates and through those fires for all eternity in exchange for but a few moments like this.'

'I learn so much from you, not just about the Bible and other matters of scholarship, but also about the whole meaning of life.'

'And yet there is a whole world outside these precinct walls, of which we are quite oblivious here.'

'I know. As a child I saw how hard life was for my family, for my brothers and sisters, and oh, how I longed to live behind these holy walls.'

'And now you are here inside these walls with me.'

'At least we can move about from one place to another, unlike Sister Odelina.'

'Yet she is blessed with visions, whereas we can only see what is here with us.'

'So let us not waste a minute of our time together.'

They began to make love again.

After the guests had broken their fasts they attended Terce, the service of prayers and singing two hours after Prime, the service at daybreak. It was early enough for Hubert, although the monks had already celebrated Matins and Lauds in the darkest hours of the night.

It was a strange experience to be in the church of Saint Gilbert, for they were aware of the great dividing wall which was painted with images of miracles performed by Christ, and of the martyrdom of various saints, including that of Saint Gilbert.

The monks and novices took their position in the choir, the area of the church before the altar where they sang their Gregorian chants in Latin, unaccompanied by music, the tones and melodies supplied entirely by the singers' voices.

Hubert, Rupert and Simon joined the brothers further back in the church. Rupert impressed all around by joining in with some of the chants that he was familiar with, his voice equal to any within the choir.

As they sang, they could hear the female voices of the nuns and lay sisters behind the dividing wall of the church. When the chanting was finished, the monks sat down on the misericords on the outer side of the church while the brothers and the guests sat on pews at right angles to them.

Prior Dominic was visible at the head of the church, as was the high altar, and as they listened they could hear the voice of the Mother Superior addressing her nuns and sisters, alternating with Prior Dominic as they shared the taking of the service.

Afterwards, the monks and brothers filtered out of the rear door of the church back into the monastery to begin their day's activities before the next service of Sext at midday.

The prior signalled for the three guests to join him in the presbytery. 'I heard you singing last night,' he said to Rupert. 'I believe everyone in the precinct did.'

Rupert smiled. 'I hope that they approved of my music?'

Prior Dominic did not reply as he led them through the part of the church called the sanctuary to the base of the high altar. The dividing wall ended here and they walked across in front of the altar to find themselves in the nun's half of the church. The wall here was also painted, yet by different hands and with depictions of martyrdoms of female saints, including Apollonia and Agnes.

The space was empty, as the nuns and sisters had already left. Then they heard soft footsteps from the far end and, turning, they saw a woman approaching. Behind her, with her head bowed, was one of the lay sisters.

The Mother Superior was a slim woman, even in her habit and scapular. She did not wear a veil, and Hubert noted that she was probably in her mid-forties. She smiled warmly as she advanced upon them.

'Mother Griselda, I have brought our guests to see you,' Prior Dominic said, introducing Hubert and Rupert. 'Friar Simon, of course, you know well.'

They all bowed and the Mother Superior stared at Rupert for a moment.

'Are you trying to see if I have a demon inside me, Mother Griselda?' Rupert asked. 'Father Robert looked last evening and saw nothing in my pupils.'

Mother Griselda smiled. 'I was looking into your eyes to see the goodness in your soul, my son.'

'And what did you see, Mother Griselda?' Rupert asked with some desperation. 'Is there goodness in my soul, or does a demon sleep inside me?'

'I see goodness in you, my son, just as I see goodness in every person.' She smiled. 'And there must be goodness in someone who sings as sweetly as you do. I enjoyed your songs last night.'

Rupert smiled at her and glanced at the prior, who said nothing. Instead, he pointed to the stone wall behind the high altar. 'Sister Odelina's cell is behind that wall. She is able to see through a squint hole if she so wishes.' Turning to the Mother Superior, he said, 'I have told our guests that we may be able to talk to Sister Odelina today.'

Mother Griselda pursed her lips. 'I regret that will not be possible.' She turned and gestured for the lay sister to step forward. 'This is Sister Patience, who is Sister Odelina's main helper. She brings fresh food and water, and sees to her laundry and personal matters.'

The young lay sister did a half curtsy. She did not look at any of them but kept her head bowed and her eyes averted.

'Do not be shy, Patience,' Mother Griselda said kindly. 'Just tell Prior Dominic what Sister Odelina said to you this morning when you attended her.'

'She … she said that she needed to talk to Mother Griselda and that she would be the only person she would talk to today. And … and —'

Mother Griselda put a reassuring hand on her shoulder. 'Well done, Patience. Go on, what else did she say?'

'She said that she would have to pray hard all day ... because ... because she has seen that something evil has come to the priory.'

There was a stunned silence while Mother Griselda dismissed Sister Patience back to her duties.

As the lay sister departed with small, quick steps down the nave of the church, Mother Griselda turned to the prior.

'I have spoken with Sister Odelina. She said her angel had told her that there is some evil presence here in the priory, but she would not be more precise. That is why she is spending the day in prayer.'

'Do you think she was referring to me?' Rupert asked, his eyes wide. 'That she could feel a demon inside me?'

Friar Simon put a comforting hand on his shoulder. 'If she did, then you must have faith that Prior Dominic and Mother Griselda will do whatever is needed to get it out of you. Have faith, my son.'

Without disturbing the anchoress in her cell, Mother Griselda and Prior Dominic led the guests on a tour of the nunnery. Like the monks and the brothers, the nuns and sisters were occupied with many tasks, ranging from the mundane and manual to the profound and spiritual, all completed in silence or with a minimal number of words.

As they went round the cloister, entering building after building, Mother Griselda introduced the guests, explaining that Master Rupert Bisley was a minstrel and that he had come to the priory under the care of Prior Dominic for rest, religious instruction and treatment of a malady he had been afflicted with. She did not allude to what exactly that was.

'I do not wish to alarm them unnecessarily,' she explained as she led them on.

The nunnery was almost identical to the monastery, but with some exceptions. The kitchen where the lay sisters cooked with supervision from nuns was vast and was run with great efficiency. Their chapter house was also larger, and there was a place where nuns could be disciplined.

'But it is seldom used,' Mother Griselda explained. 'Our sisters are all devout women and they have the ability to punish themselves, which is a far preferable arrangement for all concerned.'

When Hubert looked puzzled, she made a motion as if whipping her back with an invisible *flagellum*.

'Our scriptorium is not as well used as that of the monks, and all the work that is done here has to be examined and assessed by Father Christopher.' She opened the door to a small room off the library. Two nuns were busy with coloured inks working on illuminations that were partially completed. 'Each illumination can take many days, if not weeks.'

'Most of the scholarly work of the priory is carried out by the monks,' Prior Dominic told them. 'Although, as you can see here, Mother Griselda has many very able and artistic nuns who illuminate manuscripts, which add to our collection in the monastery library.'

They followed Mother Griselda and saw that the grounds within the precinct walls that surrounded the whole priory were extensive. The nunnery had its own granary, mill, and hospital.

'Sister Elfreda is in charge of the infirmary,' Mother Griselda said, smiling at an elderly nun as they entered the long L-shaped ward with some twenty occupied beds. 'As well as our own nuns and sisters, we accept women from the surrounding villages and hamlets who come to us for aid.'

'Do you have women in labour?' Hubert asked.

Sister Elfreda nodded. 'We have six sisters skilled in midwifery.'

Hubert smiled. 'I have four children myself and I have always said a prayer of thanks when they entered the world.'

'Sadly not all births have such a happy outcome,' said Mother Griselda. 'Our cemetery has a section for the poor souls who do not stay in this world for long.'

'And all receive baptism before burial so that they can ascend to heaven as they should,' said Sister Elfreda.

Mother Griselda led them into a small chapel attached to the hospital and opened a wooden chest in front of the altar. She pointed to a rolled parchment, made up of sheepskin squares sewn together.

'This is the birth girdle that our sisters made and gave to Sister Odelina, when she was with child from an angel. It is inscribed with prayers and images of Saints Margaret and Veronica. The child was taken by the angel and Sister Odelina was left as if she had never been pregnant.'

Sister Elfreda nodded emphatically. 'I was there that morning and there was no child, no sign that she had ever been with child, although we had all seen her belly grow. It was a miracle.'

The elderly nun genuflected before the birth girdle as Mother Griselda spoke. 'The girdle continues to perform miracles, as we have seen so many times. When wrapped around someone who has a malady, it has cured them.'

Rupert suddenly put a hand to his forehead, which had started to form beads of perspiration.

'Forgive me, but I do not feel well. I need to get into the fresh air.'

'You do indeed look pale. Come with me,' Prior Dominic said, taking his arm. 'I will take you outside and then we will go to the monastery hospital so that Father Robert can look at you.'

Hubert took his other arm and they had just left the infirmary when a lay sister came running to them from the direction of the farm where they tended their livestock.

It was Sister Patience.

'Mother Griselda!' she cried, holding her habit up so that she did not trip. 'I went to collect the … the eggs. It's dreadful! The hens — five of them are dead.'

'Was it a fox, Patience?' Mother Griselda asked in alarm.

'No, Mother, it must have been a … a person. They have had their heads cut off and are laid out in … in a pattern.'

'Perhaps that is the evil that Sister Odelina sensed,' Prior Dominic said softly.

15

Hubert left Rupert with Prior Dominic and Friar Simon and went with Mother Griselda and Sister Patience to the farm.

The sight that greeted them when they reached the hen run made Mother Griselda put her hand to her mouth and gasp. Several hens were running back and forth against the enclosure wall, clucking and squawking in panic.

In the centre of the hen run were the five severed heads, their bodies discarded in a heap at the far end. The heads had been laid out in the form of a five-pointed star that had been gouged into the soft ground. The star itself was enclosed in a circle.

'It is a pentagram,' said Mother Griselda, putting an arm about Patience's shoulders. 'You did the correct thing, my dear. Now go inside to the kitchen and have some milk. It will calm you.'

When the lay sister had gone she looked at Hubert, who had let himself into the hen run and had found another five-pointed star inside a circle. This one drawn was in blood on the side of the hen house.

'It is an evil sign, Master Hubert. It is of the Dark Arts!'

'Yes, but a priory is the last place that I would have expected to find such a thing.'

'It will have to be removed and the dead hens burned,' Mother Griselda said. 'I will get one of the sisters to do it.'

Thinking that he should examine the scene further, Hubert said, 'With respect, Mother Griselda, I do not think it is a job for your sisters. May I suggest that I do it along with one of the monks?'

The Mother Superior pursed her lips in thought. 'Perhaps you are right. In any case, Prior Dominic must be informed.'

Returning to the nunnery, Mother Griselda was informed by Sister Enid that the guest who had arrived the night before wished to meet with her and the two male guests who were staying in the monastery hospitium. They all wished to consult with Sister Odelina afterwards.

Mother Griselda clasped her hands together and turned to Hubert. 'I must see to my distinguished guest and inform her that Sister Odelina cannot be disturbed today. Sister Enid here will escort you back to the church so that you can return to the monastery to see how Master Bisley is faring. And if you would be so kind as to inform Prior Dominic about the hens?'

Back in the hospital, Rupert had been given a draught of medicine by Father Robert and had recovered his colour, he looked sleepy.

'I do not know what came over me, Master Hubert,' he said as he lay yawning on his cot. Father Robert and Friar Simon were standing looking down at him.

'Did it feel as if one of your attacks was coming on?' Father Robert asked.

The minstrel shook his head. 'It was the sight of the birth girdle. I felt as if I would vomit, but I know not why.'

'Many things can trigger nausea,' said Father Robert. 'Perhaps it was the odour of the parchment, or —'

'Or the power of the holy words that had been written on it?' suggested Friar Simon.

Rupert looked up at them all anxiously. 'You are saying that the demon inside me didn't like seeing the girdle?'

'That is likely, I believe,' said Simon.

'What do you think, Father Robert?' Hubert asked.

The hospitaller scratched his chin. 'I am not sure. It is possible, I admit, but —'

'But what?' Rupert asked urgently, sitting up on his cot.

'But that would mean that it can see through your eyes.'

'Yet you said you could see nothing in my eyes.'

'I said it might be sleeping.'

The minstrel let out a sigh. 'When will you know if I truly have a demon inside me? And when will something be done about it?'

'That is for Prior Dominic to decide,' Father Robert said, spreading his hands out in a gesture of helplessness.

'Ah, where is the prior? I must see him,' said Hubert.

Rupert yawned again and his eyes started to look heavy. 'I dimly remember the sister coming with an urgent message as he and Friar Simon were helping me back...' He trailed off.

Father Robert smiled. 'The draught I gave him is working well. He will be asleep in a few moments.'

Hubert said, 'May I speak with you both in private?'

Father Robert nodded and led them into the dispensary where he compounded his medicines. There, Hubert told them of the slaughtered hens and the two pentagrams that had appeared in the hen run.

'That is most unsettling news, Hubert,' said Friar Simon, making the sign of the cross. 'It does indeed sound as if evil has entered the priory.'

With raised eyebrows the hospitaller added, 'The question is whether you brought it with you?'

'So, where is the prior?' Hubert asked.

'I was informed that two distinguished guests in the hospitium had arranged to meet with a female guest in the nunnery guest house before seeing Sister Odelina this morning.

You will either find him in the hospitium or he will be conveying them to the nunnery.'

'Do you know who these dignified guests are?'

Father Robert nodded. 'One is my Lord Bishop of Durham, Lewis de Beaumont, and the other is the Earl of Lancaster.'

Hubert was grateful when Simon offered to accompany him to the hospitium, which was situated within the monastery physic garden close to the cloister. Although he had met many nobles during his service with Sir Richard, he was still conscious of his relatively low position. Simon, as a friar of the Franciscan Order, had no such reservations. He asked for alms from those of all stations in life without any qualms.

As they entered the outer chamber of the hospitium, they were met by the young monk Father Luke. He was studying a scroll as they entered and rose to his feet with the vigour of youth and a welcoming smile.

'May I help you, my friends?'

'I need to talk to Prior Dominic,' Hubert said. 'It is an urgent matter about something that has occurred in the nunnery.'

'Prior Dominic is about to escort our distinguished guests to the nunnery. Can it wait?'

'It would be prudent —' Simon began.

At that moment the door to the inner hall of the hospitium opened and the Earl of Lancaster and the Bishop of Durham entered, followed by Prior Dominic.

The bishop was helping to guide the earl, who had his eyes screwed up, as one who had difficulty seeing. The earl, in turn, was supporting his fellow guest, who was hobbling on both feet.

Hubert and Simon bowed and the two dignitaries nodded without interest.

Prior Dominic frowned. 'Have you come to tell me of that matter in the nunnery?' He raised an eyebrow in a conspiratorial manner that Hubert immediately interpreted to mean that he should say nothing to alarm his noble guests.

'I have, my lord,' Hubert replied deferentially.

'I am about to lead our guests to see Mother Griselda. In the meanwhile, perhaps you could tell Father Luke about it and then he can discuss it with me afterwards when he has my ear.'

At Hubert's nod he left the hospitium, followed by the two dignitaries. Father Luke closed the door behind them and turned to face Hubert and Simon.

'So, what can I help you with?'

Hubert looked at Simon, then began. 'When we and Master Rupert Bisley were being shown around the nunnery —'

'Master Bisley is the minstrel that I heard play so beautifully last night? He is here to receive healing from either the birth girdle or Saint Gilbert's finger, I understand.'

'That is so, but when Sister Elfreda showed us the birth girdle, Rupert was taken ill. We were taking him back to the hospital in the monastery when Sister Patience came to tell Mother Griselda that she had found five hens had been decapitated.'

Father Luke drew back in alarm. 'You mean they had their heads cut off?'

'Aye, and arranged in a pattern. Mother Griselda called it a pentagram.'

'Surely a sign that something evil is going on here,' said Simon.

The young monk looked even more shocked. 'Not in the priory. That is not possible. We are a house of the Lord.'

'Yet there is more,' Hubert went on. 'The same symbol is painted in blood on the hen house. Mother Griselda wants it removed and the dead chickens burned, but I think that we should examine it further. That is certainly what my master, Sir Richard Lee, would do. The prior should see it as well.'

Father Luke nodded. 'I agree we should go and see it. But I would suggest that we also bring Father Christopher as he is well versed in all manner of art, illustration and symbology, and also Father Joseph who has knowledge of books on all subjects in our library.'

'Even of the Dark Arts?' Hubert asked.

'I believe so.'

Sister Enid had been told to wait in the nun's side of the church by Mother Griselda while she attended to her distinguished guest in the guest house. The elderly sister escorted Hubert, Simon and the three monks through to their infirmary where they asked her to wait while they went to the hen house.

'Have any of you seen such a thing before?' Hubert asked.

'I certainly have never witnessed anything so horrible,' said Father Luke.

'But I have,' Father Joseph interjected. 'We have several texts in the library on the occult.'

'You mean on the Dark Arts, Father?' Simon asked.

'I do, and in them there are depictions of various symbols used in ceremonies that are not religious.'

'I too have seen illustrations of this device,' said Father Christopher. 'There are the two triangles within a circle, which is called the Star of Solomon. It is formed by drawing two triangles on top of each other so that it produces a six-pointed star. It is also called a hexagram. But this is a pentagram, meaning it has five points. It can be a sign of the rising Lord if it has only one point at the top. But when there are two, like this, it is a sign of Satan himself, for they are like his horns.'

'And with the hen heads placed on each point, there is little doubt that it has been used in some evil ceremony,' said Hubert.

'I think it needs to be removed, the bodies and heads burned and the whole area blessed and dowsed with holy water,' said Father Joseph. 'As soon as possible.'

Father Christopher was scrutinising the symbol painted upon the hen house with his magnifying glass. 'Interesting,' he muttered. 'Not exactly the work of an illustrator, but a crude daub. I'd say it was done by pressing the bloody head or the neck of a hen and using it like a brush.'

Hubert looked over his shoulder. 'I see what you mean. There seem to be bits of flesh caught on the splinters of wood.'

Father Luke had knelt down to look at the decapitated heads. He gingerly pointed to two of them. 'It looks as if these were the ones used, as they have splinters of wood stuck in them.'

Father Christopher knelt down beside Father Luke and inspected the heads with his magnifying glass. Then he abruptly stood up. 'Yet what use could knowing that be?' he said sharply. 'I agree with Joseph; we should have this all dealt with.'

'I also think that we should not talk about this other than to Prior Dominic — it could alarm everyone,' said Father Joseph.

'I agree,' said Father Luke. 'And I shall get holy water and bless this area to drive the evil out.'

'All three of us should do it,' said Father Joseph to the two other monks. 'The triangle is a sign of divinity and our combined blessing will be more powerful.'

'Then we will leave you to it,' Hubert said. 'I will go and see how Master Bisley is doing.'

Sister Enid was awaiting them at the infirmary and escorted them back to the church.

'So, Hubert,' Simon began, having been quiet while they inspected the hen house. 'Do you think that someone held a Dark Art ceremony there?'

'I don't think so,' Hubert replied. 'I can't see what the purpose would be. Rather, I think it was someone leaving a message for some reason. But who and why?'

How I wish that Sir Richard was here, he thought as they made their way back to the monastery hospital.

Mother Griselda made her private parlour available to Lady Isabella de Vesci, Lewis de Beaumont, the Bishop of Durham, and Henry, the Earl of Lancaster. She and Prior Dominic stood apart from the seated dignitaries.

'Mother Griselda here tells us that Sister Odelina will not talk to anyone, not even us, until tomorrow,' Lady Isabella said, addressing Prior Dominic.

The prior nodded. 'That is correct, my lady. She will hear you after Terce in the morning, when she will bless the birth girdle and use it to bless yourselves and another who is in need of healing.'

The Earl of Lancaster grunted irritably. 'Time is of the essence. I require healing, yet I am also here to look for guidance from Sister Odelina and urgently need her to commune with her angel on our behalf. I need a sign from the divine to reassure me that the path we have embarked on is still the correct and just one.'

'It no longer seems right,' said Lewis de Beaumont. 'Edmund of Woodstock is dead. Our King Edward the Second must be dead and his son, King Edward, who sits on the throne, is in peril at this very moment. Which means that so too is his queen and his newborn heir.'

Lady Isabella turned to Mother Griselda and Prior Dominic. 'Do either of you know if the messenger that was sent with our mission has any information that we should know about?'

'The messenger did not report on anything that you do not already know, my lady,' said Prior Dominic.

'And did they talk to anyone else?' Lewis asked. 'Did they give any information that could lead to us?'

'No, they knew that it could mean death. Not just for them, but for countless others.'

'And it must remain so,' Lady Isabella said emphatically. 'Especially now.'

Earl Henry blinked repeatedly as he tried to focus on the Mother Superior and the prior. 'What about all your nuns and sisters, and the monks and brothers? Are they aware of what has happened?'

'They are aware that the Earl of Kent was executed after being found guilty of treason against the king,' Prior Dominic replied.

'Pah! I meant about the message we sent,' he snapped irritably.

'And what about the messenger?' said the bishop. 'We three have never even met this person, which I for one am not happy about.'

'I agree,' said Lady Isabella. 'We have put our trust in someone we have never set eyes upon.'

'Not that I would have seen much of them in any case,' grumbled Earl Henry.

Mother Griselda shared a look with Prior Dominic. 'We trust this person implicitly, my lords and lady. We felt that it would be safest for all concerned if you did not know this person, in case anything happened in these very troubled days.'

'But does anyone here at the priory know that this person is in any way connected with us?'

'No,' Prior Dominic replied. 'All here would have been aware that some in our number were abroad on business of the priory, but not what that business was.' He gave a wry smile. 'There are advantages to the near-silent life that we lead in the order. When people talk as little as we, few secrets are ever divulged.'

'Except during confession,' Mother Griselda volunteered.

'And I decide who will hear another's confession,' Prior Dominic said. 'We are extremely good at keeping secrets here in Cawthorne Priory.'

16

Prior Dominic listened to Father Luke's account of how he and the two older monks had disposed of the slaughtered hens and cleaned away the symbols that they had found in the hen run, before they had dowsed the whole area with holy water.

'What do you intend to do now, Prior Dominic?' Hubert asked.

'I have already discussed the situation with Mother Griselda. Since this desecration occurred in the nunnery, her opinion was most important.'

'And what did she think should be done, my lord?' Friar Simon asked.

'She has been to consult with Sister Odelina.'

'But I understood that she was not to be disturbed this day?' Simon said with a small frown. 'She wished to spend the day in prayer.'

'That is so, but the immensity of this outrage was such that we both felt we had to intrude on Sister Odelina's seclusion.'

'May we know what she said, Prior Dominic?' Father Christopher asked.

'Indeed, you may. She already knew of it.'

The three monks, Hubert and Friar Simon all stared in amazement.

'Had … had she been told by her angel?' Father Joseph asked.

'No, she had been told by Sister Patience when she had taken her plate away and passed through a fresh habit and underclothes.'

'And did she give counsel about the sacrilege?' Father Christopher queried.

'She said that she had already told Sister Patience to let it be known among the nuns and sisters. That they all had a right to be informed that evil had entered the nunnery and that they should all pray and purge themselves.'

'Purge themselves?' Hubert repeated. 'You mean —'

'Purge themselves of sin by flagellation and purge themselves of evil by internal cleansing.'

'But was that not for Mother Griselda to decide?' Father Joseph asked, aghast.

'Indeed, and yet so great is Mother Griselda's respect for Sister Odelina that she acquiesced. Sister Patience passed the message from Sister Odelina directly to Sister Enid and the other senior nuns, who then passed it on to the community. Sister Elfreda is busily making aperient draughts to distribute to the community at this very moment. The Mother Superior has also instructed the lay sisters to ensure that the reredorter latrines in the nunnery are ready and that the water supply from the stream is running smoothly.'

'How have the nuns and the sisters taken the news, my lord?' Father Luke asked.

'They are fearful, as you would imagine.'

'And young Sister Patience?' Father Joseph asked with concern. 'Is she very upset?'

'As upset as all are about the sacrilege that has taken place. We are going to follow Sister Odelina's advice and inform the monks and brothers. There shall be no purging, however. But we shall all pray that the culprit reveals herself.'

'You believe the perpetrator to be a woman?' Simon asked, eyebrows raised.

'It happened in the nunnery,' Prior Dominic replied simply.

'Would you like me to help?' Hubert asked. 'I know Sir Richard Lee's methods and could —'

Prior Dominic smiled. 'Your prayers will be welcomed, too, my son.'

The rest of the day continued as usual in the priory, and yet Hubert had the impression that all seemed ill at ease.

As the monk charged with overseeing the pilgrims, Father Luke was one of the few monks who talked as he carried out his duties. Hubert and Simon saw him leading a group of ailing pilgrims from the undercroft to the small pilgrim's chapel near the precinct wall. He was walking at their head and answering a question from one.

'I regret to say that Prior Dominic has decreed that we may not show the relic of Saint Gilbert at this time,' he replied to the pilgrim.

'What about the birth girdle?' asked a man who was bent almost double, wearing a robe and a liripipe hat. 'A neighbour of mine said that he had been cured of bladder stones by having it wrapped around his belly. I had hoped to gain similar comfort for my lameness.'

Father Luke shook his head. 'I am afraid that it is kept in the nunnery, and I have been told that it is also not available at this time outside of our regular services.'

Turning, he led the party into the chapel after him.

Hubert looked around to ensure that they were out of earshot of anyone. 'I feel uneasy about this, Friar Simon. I cannot understand why the Prior and the Mother Superior are just hoping that the person responsible will simply confess and ask for forgiveness. I have seen enough of the real world to know that people who do bad things are loath to ever own up.'

Simon nodded. 'It is concerning, I admit, but this is a whole community based on faith. They do not wish to even consider that one of their own could do such a thing and not be ridden with guilt.'

'But surely they can see that someone meant for the atrocity to be found? It is hardly something that would be done as a jest.'

On Hubert's suggestion they made their way to the library, where they found several monks studying books at desks and noisily scratching notes on vellum. Knocking on the door of the librarian's inner office, they found both Father Joseph and Father Christopher bent over a leatherbound book laid open on the large desk, which was home to a crucifix, a huge hourglass, an astrolabe and various other obscure pieces of apparatus. Father Christopher was examining a diagram in the book through his magnifying glass.

'Ah, Hubert of Loxley and Friar Simon, we have found it,' Father Joseph said as they approached the desk. 'Here is the Great Grimoire of Ambrosius Sartorius, which has been in the library for all the time that I have lived here. It was written over a hundred years ago by my estimation, and it is an instructional book of demonology.'

'Not a well written or well constructed book, in my opinion,' said Father Christopher, letting his glass slip from his hand to dangle from his neck on its leather strap. 'We were just looking at the illustrations, which are crudely drawn.'

Friar Simon leaned close. 'The ink is a strange colour, is it not?'

'We think it is blood, which is why it looks so dark,' Father Joseph remarked.

'Human?' Hubert asked in disgust.

'Who could tell?' Father Christopher replied. 'But we take no chances, hence this large crucifix at our side. But you see the diagram. It is exactly as that symbol was drawn.'

'Who could have access to this book?' Hubert asked.

'Any of the monks or brothers,' replied Father Joseph.

'But what about the nuns and sisters?'

Both monks shook their heads.

'It is unlikely that there would be a book like this in the nun's library, for it is a much smaller place,' Father Joseph volunteered.

Hubert and Simon exchanged glances.

Prior Dominic was not present at the evening meal in the refectory. Father Jacob, the bucolic-looking steward who looked after the priory's administration and business affairs, took his place in reading the biblical text before bread was broken and food was served. Hubert thought by the slur in his voice and the increased ruddiness of his nose and cheeks that he had been imbibing wine throughout the afternoon.

Father Barnabas the choirmaster sat morosely throughout the meal, barely touching his food, and altogether there was far less banter and chatter than previously.

'This is a most surly gathering for supper,' said Rupert Bisley in a hushed voice. He was sitting between Hubert and Simon.

'They all know about the desecration in the nunnery,' Hubert whispered.

'But what exactly did you see?' Rupert asked. 'Father Robert would not talk about it in the hospital, and there are all sorts of rumours going around the other patients. I was so drowsy all day from that draught the good hospitaller gave me that I barely caught much of it.'

'Well, I do not think we will hear anyone speaking about it this evening,' said Simon. 'Perhaps we can talk in the cloister later.'

The evening was cold, but as usual the design of the cloister protected those within from the winds, and the lanterns that were lit all around the enclosed walkway gave out a warm glow. Hubert, Rupert and Simon walked briskly round the cloister to keep warm while Hubert described all that had happened that day.

'It sounds wicked indeed,' said Rupert. 'And it seems to me that it was designed to spread alarm. Whether it had any devilish effect, who can tell?' He gave a rueful laugh. 'The demon in me certainly hasn't been stirred up by their antics.' He patted his lute. 'This is a most unhappy place this night, and some music might lift the mood of those within hearing.'

The minstrel played and sang as they walked. Hubert and Simon both smiled as the music carried on the night air.

The door of the cell was pushed closed, and they faced one another.

'I had to come.'

'You should not have. It was a dangerous thing to do. Especially with all that has happened.'

'But I needed to be with you. To know how you feel. I want to lie with you.'

Hands made to lift the habit, but were stayed.

'No! We must wait now.'

'I need you to prove that you love me.'

And this time no effort was made to stop the wandering hands.

The continual drip of the water clocks, and the fall of sand in the hourglasses in the dormitories and cells marked the slow passage of time. Few in the order slept well as night advanced and the Matins was celebrated.

Those that did manage to sleep did so only fitfully.

Sister Odelina was one such. She woke in the pitch darkness of her cell and felt her heart pounding in her chest. She reached to touch the crucifix that hung between her breasts and muttered a silent prayer. There was evil around her, that she knew. But now she felt that it was nearby.

Then she heard her angel's voice and suddenly her fear disappeared. Her angel would not permit danger to come to her.

'Odelina! Odelina!' the voice called softly.

'Yes, I am here. What must I do?'

'Nothing for now! But you must watch the services this day through your squint hole and if you see evil, you must denounce it at once.'

'But what form will —'

'You will see that there are fornicators in their midst. Many of them. You must act immediately.'

'Act how?'

'Tell them all. They must purge themselves of their sins.'

'But —'

'I must leave you now, Odelina,' the voice said, softer as if more distant. 'Farewell.'

'No! No! Are you there? Please, please come back.'

She stood and put her ear to the squint hole, but heard nothing.

Her angel was gone.

The lay sisters' dormitory had a single burning candle at each end. Twenty sisters lay in the cots against each wall.

The moaning noise was horrible and roused every sister from her slumber. Some pulled their blankets over their heads. Others dared to raise their heads from their straw pillows, and a few of the bravest sat up as the sound of feet pounded on the dormitory floor and the moaning became louder.

Halfway along the dormitory Sister Patience, not one of the brave, but curious enough to sit up, screamed at the sight of the nun in full dress, reeling and staggering and gesticulating wildly.

'He comes! He has me and he will take you!' the nun cried out in a terrible voice. 'Purge! Purge! Purge!'

Sisters dashed from their cots, seeking comfort in the cots of their neighbours or friends.

And then the moaning turned into a maniacal deep-throated laughter as the nun whirled and jerked before their horrified eyes, finally crashing through the door, which slammed closed behind her.

Then they all started screaming.

Mother Griselda was wakened from her sleep by Sister Elfreda and informed of what had happened in the lay sisters' dormitory.

'Who was the nun?' she demanded.

'We don't know, Mother. We were all in our cells. Five of the sisters came together for safety to rouse us and tell us about the ghost.'

'Ghost! They think it was a ghost?'

'They all think it was an evil spirit or the tormented ghost of a nun, but no one knew her, Mother Griselda. And they are all saying that it was because of that … that evil thing that was done yesterday.'

'There are no ghosts in my nunnery. I shall come and reassure them all.' She threw back her blanket before adding, 'And Sister Elfreda, there must be no mention of this before our distinguished guests, who will be at the service later this morning.'

Mother Griselda informed Prior Dominic of the night's events before Terce.

'Should we inform Sister Odelina of this?' she asked.

'No, I think not. But it would be sensible to tell Hubert of Loxley and the monks.'

'I told Sister Patience to make no mention of it, so if Sister Odelina knows then it can only be from her angel.'

The service was conducted as planned. Lady Isabella sat on a chair in front of the choir on the nunnery side of the church, and the Bishop of Durham and the Earl of Lancaster sat in similar position on the monastery side.

Behind the monastery choir, Hubert, Friar Simon and Rupert Bisley stood in front of the lay brothers. At the very back of the church, the group of pilgrims had been permitted to stand in attendance.

Hymns were sung, psalms were read and doleful Gregorian chants from both the nunnery and monastery sides echoed around the church, producing a strange mixture of soprano, baritone and bass voices.

Then Prior Dominic, standing at the lectern, read a lesson from the Gospel according to Mark, chapter five.

'The Lord encountered a man who lived among the tombs, possessed by numerous demons. When Jesus commanded the unclean spirits to come out

of the man, the demons begged him not to send them out of the country but into a nearby herd of pigs. Jesus granted their request, and the demons entered the pigs, causing them to rush into the sea and drown.'

Rupert prodded Hubert. 'That was especially for me,' he whispered. 'Do you think they are going to get some pigs ready for my demon?'

Hubert forced a smile. He admired the minstrel's ability to maintain some humour, even when faced with the unknown.

'Witness what is next to come,' Prior Dominic intoned. 'We have three distinguished guests and the minstrel Rupert Bisley. They are here for healing with the birth girdle of Sister Odelina, which is known to have miraculous powers and which you have all witnessed before. I now ask Mother Griselda and Sister Elfreda to bring the casket with the birth girdle forth and we shall begin.'

Rupert walked to the front of the choir and stood a couple of paces behind the seated bishop and earl.

The Mother Superior and Sister Elfreda came into view before the altar, Mother Griselda with her hands together and Sister Elfreda bearing the casket.

Sister Elfreda turned to face Mother Griselda, who opened the lid. She looked inside and then shrieked.

'What...?' Prior Dominic stammered. He walked forward two paces and put his hands in the casket, drawing out two handfuls of shredded sheepskin parchment and holding it up in disgust. Upon the vellum was a crudely daubed red pentagram inside a circle.

'The sign of devilry!'

Suddenly, Rupert clutched his throat and made a horrible gurgling noise. All about him stared in horror as he began to shake violently. Spittle formed on his lips and then he collapsed, writing and kicking on the floor in front of the altar.

'Evil! I see evil!' screamed a voice from behind the altar wall.

'It is Sister Odelina,' gasped Sister Elfreda.

'I see evil!' the disembodied voice of the anchoress screeched from her cell. 'I see fornicators in your midst.'

Lady Isabella, the Bishop of Durham and the Earl of Lancaster all looked aghast.

'Do something, in God's name!' cried the bishop.

'You must all be purged! Purge yourselves!' came the voice.

Rupert continued to convulse as Father Robert dashed to him with a crucifix in his hand.

Hubert had gone to assist the hospitaller and was relieved to see that after some minutes of violent thrashing the fit subsided and Father Robert felt able to release Rupert's tongue, which he had held down with the crucifix.

Suddenly a lay brother whose name was Brother Walter came running in through the door at the back of the monastery side of the church. 'Help me! Help me! It's Father Christopher, I … I found him —'

Hubert ran to him and grasped the brother by the shoulders. 'What do you mean, Brother? You found him where?'

'In … in his cell. He's dead. He … he has hanged himself.'

The nuns on the other side of the wall started to wail and cry while the brothers behind the choir crossed themselves in fear.

Leaving Rupert to recover in the care of Sister Elfreda while Prior Dominic and Mother Griselda did their best to calm everyone down, Hubert and Father Robert followed Brother Walter through the cloister and up the stairs to the monks' cells. Throwing open the door, they saw the body of Father

Christopher hanging from a rafter by a rope. His face was purple, his eyes bulged, and his swollen tongue protruded from his mouth. A stool lay on its side on the floor beneath his dangling feet. His red leather shoes lay on the floor.

'Let us get him down to see if he yet lives,' said Father Robert.

Hubert pulled out his knife and handed it to the monk. 'You cut the rope while I lift him.'

Grabbing his legs, Hubert hoisted the monk upwards enough for the rope to slacken and for Father Robert to cut it. As they carried the body to the cot and laid it down, they saw that the rope had actually been threaded through the leather strap from which the monk suspended his magnifying glass.

'He had twisted this strap and wrapped it round his neck and then threaded the rope through before tying it to the beam,' said Father Robert as he pulled the rope free and unwound the leather strap from his neck. 'He must have wanted to use the leather that held the glass he has used these last few years.'

'Is he dead?' Hubert asked.

'He looks to have been for many hours,' Father Robert replied.

Brother Walter was standing with his back pressed against the wall. At this pronouncement he let out a strangled sob.

The sound of running feet was heard outside then Friar Simon came in. He was breathing heavily after his exertion.

'The Lord have mercy upon his soul,' he said, making the sign of the cross. 'Why would he do such a thing?'

'That is what I must find out,' said Hubert. 'But first we must send a messenger to Sandal Castle. My master, Sir Richard Lee, must come and investigate.'

The door creaked open behind them, and Hubert spun round to see the pilgrim who had looked so bent when he had seen him the day before. Only now he was no longer bent, but stood straight and tall. He pulled off the liripipe hat that shrouded his face.

'There is no need for a messenger, Hubert. I am here, and it looks as though the things I feared would happen have already begun.'

17

Hubert stared in astonishment.

'How … how long have you been here, my lord?'

Richard saw the stunned look on Hubert's face and patted his arm. 'Almost as long as yourself, Hubert. But it was important that no one should know of my presence, until this dreadful crime.'

'Self-killing is a mortal sin!' said Friar Simon, who looked almost as surprised to see Richard as Hubert.

'But who are you?' Father Robert demanded. 'If you are not the pilgrim Judson of Newbold that you claimed to be?'

'I am Sir Richard Lee, Circuit Judge of the King's Northern Realm and Coroner to Wakefield and the five towns around.'

'This is my master,' added Hubert.

Richard knelt by the cot to examine Father Christopher's body. He ran his hands over the torso and abdomen.

'No signs of wounding,' he said to no one in particular. He pushed up the sleeves of his habit and the clothing underneath. 'And no evidence of a fight, no bruising or scratches.'

'Why are you looking for such things?' asked Father Robert. 'It is clear that he has hanged himself. Although I know not why.'

Brother Walter let out another loud sob. Hubert turned to him and, seeing the tears streaming down his face, rested a hand gently on his shoulder. 'You are distressed, Brother. Why don't you spare yourself any further sight of this and get some fresh air? We will seek you later.'

Walter nodded and left the cell as Richard began examining the bruising about the dead monk's throat.

'This bruising is curious,' he mused. Then, standing, he addressed Hubert. 'Is there a message or anything that he has written?'

'Father Christopher was in charge of the scriptorium,' Father Robert volunteered, pointing to the small desk in the corner of the cell. 'As you can see, he was a precise and methodical monk.'

A wooden crucifix hung on the wall above the desk. On the surface was an unlit candle in a holder, a pot of assorted quills, a sharpening knife and a box containing various bottles of coloured inks. A neat pile of small books including a Bible was stacked on a corner and in the middle there was a rolled-up vellum scroll.

'Unroll that scroll, Hubert,' Richard instructed. 'See what he was working on.'

As Hubert unfurled the vellum scroll, he let out a soft whistle. 'It is the same symbol we found in the nunnery, my lord!'

'And the same symbol was scrawled on some of the birth girdle pieces, unless I am mistaken,' said Richard.

'It is a pentagram inside a circle, my lord,' Hubert explained. 'Yesterday we discovered the heads of five hens had been laid out on a symbol like this etched on the ground of the hen run. The same image was also painted on the hen house. Father Christopher and Father Joseph have discovered a drawing of it in a book they called a grimoire in the library.'

'You must tell me more of this, but first I must have words with Prior Dominic and the Mother Superior. Have this door locked and leave the body undisturbed in the meantime.'

In Mother Griselda's parlour Lady Isabella, her brother Lewis de Beaumont and Earl Henry sat looking shocked and disgruntled. Mother Griselda, Prior Dominic and Richard were standing, but there was no doubt that it was Richard who had taken command of the proceedings.

They had all been surprised when he had announced who he was and revealed the official seal of office.

'There has been much malevolence carried out these past few days,' said Richard now. 'And I suspect that the priory's three distinguished patrons have not been aware of it.'

'We most certainly have not!' said Lady Isabella. 'And I for one am most displeased.'

'We came here to consult with the anchoress and receive healing for the maladies that we have been afflicted with,' Earl Henry stated bluntly. 'This morning in the church we saw that sacrilege had been committed, and now it seems that madness has descended upon the whole priory.'

Bishop Lewis nodded. 'I have seen it with my own eyes and ears. The sisters are wailing and the brothers are crying out, moaning, and behaving most peculiarly. Some are barking and running like dogs. They all appear to have lost their wits!'

'I have ordered the monks to herd the brothers back to their dormitories for now,' Prior Dominic replied.

'As have I ordered my nuns to take the sisters back to theirs,' volunteered Mother Griselda.

'But we can still hear them!' snapped Lady Isabella.

'I assure you, we will settle everything, my lords and lady,' said Mother Griselda. 'We just need some time to cast this evil out.' She looked hesitantly at the prior and then accusingly at Richard. 'This madness all began when that minstrel you sent us started playing his music.'

'It is not madness, but evil,' Richard interrupted. 'And I am here to discover its source.' He stopped and looked at the prior. 'Where is Rupert Bisley, by the way?'

'Father Robert, Friar Simon and two of the brothers took him back to the hospital and under my instructions they have confiscated his instruments.'

'Well, we have decided we are leaving,' declared the bishop.

'I am afraid that will not be possible,' said Richard. 'I require everyone to remain in the priory while I conduct my investigations.'

'How dare you!' roared Earl Henry. 'Do you know who —?'

'I know exactly who you are, my lord. And that is partly why I must insist that you all stay. I understand that you are all patrons of Cawthorne Priory. Father Christopher's death may have serious implications for the priory, and it is important that I have your cooperation while I investigate it.'

Prior Dominic grunted. 'I think we would all appreciate an explanation, Sir Richard. I must confess that I feel somewhat aggrieved that you denied me the courtesy of an introduction by coming here disguised as a pilgrim.'

'I apologise. It was a necessary subterfuge so that I could observe what was happening without arousing suspicion.'

'Suspicion of what, sirrah?' snapped Earl Henry.

'That I was here to unmask someone.'

'Unmask someone?' exclaimed Lady Isabella. 'Unmask who and for what?'

'Someone who is here to cause chaos. That is as much as I may say at this stage.'

Prior Dominic and Mother Griselda stared in alarm. 'But you must tell us more. We are all grief-stricken that Father Christopher has taken his own life. It is an unforgivable sin. He will not be admitted into Heaven nor be buried in consecrated ground. Is that not chaos enough?'

'I confess that I suspected someone was going to die, but I did not know who,' Richard said. 'Unfortunately, it occurred in such a way that I could not prevent it.'

There was the sound of running feet in the corridor outside then an urgent knocking on the door.

Mother Griselda moved to open the door, but it burst open before she could reach it. Sister Enid entered, trembling. Hubert, who had been waiting outside in the corridor, followed her in.

'Mother, we … we have found Sister Helen in the laundry.'

'Is she ill?' Mother Griselda demanded.

'She is dead!'

Richard and Hubert followed Sister Enid and Mother Griselda to the laundry with its great vats and baths, baskets of habits and underclothes all kept segregated into those belonging to nuns, sisters, brothers and monks. A foul odour filled the air, emanating from baths full of urine and buckets of ash.

'Sister Helen did not sleep in her dormitory last night,' Sister Enid explained as they passed through the laundry rooms. 'It was only when the sisters were sent back to their dormitory after that awful service that we realised she was missing. So Sister Elfreda and I searched and we found her here, in the ironing room.' She ran ahead and opened a door to let them in. 'Sister Elfreda stayed with her, but there was nothing she could do.'

They entered the room with its racks of irons and saw the body of a young lay sister lying on the floor in a pool of blood. She was wearing a white scapular with a white lamb's wool headdress. The attached cotton veil had been swept upwards to reveal her face, which was frozen in an expression of horror. Her eyes were still open and staring upwards. An ugly wound was visible on each wrist and both hands were covered in blood. The right hand clasped a sharp knife.

Sister Elfreda was kneeling and seemed deep in silent prayer beside the pool of blood. At their entry she opened her eyes and looked up at them, her eyes red from crying.

'I … I wanted to close her eyes, but I thought she should not be disturbed until she was seen.'

'We shall close them now, Sister,' Mother Griselda said. 'And we shall pray for her soul after committing this sin against God.'

'No! Do not touch her,' Richard commanded. 'I must inspect the body.'

Sister Elfreda held out her hand. 'I took this from her mouth.'

It was a piece of vellum rolled into a ball. Richard unfurled it.

'It is a piece of the birth girdle!' Mother Griselda exclaimed. 'And … and it has one of those terrible pentagrams on it.'

'I thought it was an obscenity, leaving it in her mouth,' Sister Elfreda explained.

Richard pointed to the scapular and headdress. 'I understood that Sister Helen was a lay sister. Is this not a nun's scapular?'

'She was a lay sister,' Mother Griselda confirmed. 'She should not have been wearing this.'

'The sisters said a ghostly nun ran through their dormitory last night,' Hubert pointed out. 'Could it have been Sister Helen, dressed thus?'

Sister Enid's head shot up. 'And it must have been her who desecrated the birth girdle. The poor woman must have been possessed and then, realising what she had done, she — killed herself.'

Richard leaned over the body. 'I need to examine her more closely. Indeed, it would be best if you all leave. Hubert, please stay and assist me.'

Once the nuns had left, Richard made a more thorough examination of the corpse. He raised the blood-soaked sleeves to look for signs of a struggle on the hands and forearms. Then he looked under the habit and scapular at the dead woman's throat.

'There is bruising here around the neck, which is as I suspected,' he said. 'She was throttled to death and that vellum was shoved into her mouth to prevent her making any noise. When I saw how deep the wrist wounds were, I thought it would have been unlikely that she could have cut both wrists. It looks as if the tendons were sliced through, so she would have had no grip for the second wrist.'

Richard nodded as he pulled the knife from her hand. 'No, this knife was placed in her hand after her murderer had slashed through her wrists to make it look like self-killing.' He rose to his feet and scratched his chin.

'So we have two murders, my lord?' Hubert asked.

'We have. But for now it would be best if the killer is under the impression that their attempts to disguise the murders have been successful. I fear this could just be the beginning.'

<h1 style="text-align:center">18</h1>

Back in Mother Griselda's parlour Richard told the three dignitaries, Prior Dominic and the Mother Superior that because the two recent deaths had both involved violent means, an inquest would have to be held.

'But surely Canon Law overrules that since they occurred in a religious house?' argued Bishop Lewis de Beaumont.

'No, it is the law of England,' Richard replied. 'And as the King's Judge of his Northern Realm, I must investigate the deaths and then hold the inquest.'

'And just where will this inquest be held?' Lady Isabella demanded.

'At the Wodehalle in Wakefield, once I have conducted my investigations into these two deaths,' Richard returned.

'And how long will that take?' Earl Henry asked. 'I have important affairs that cannot be delayed any longer.' He gestured at Lady Isabella and the bishop. 'We all have urgent matters to deal with.'

'Which is exactly why I must begin,' Richard replied emphatically. He turned to Prior Dominic and Mother Griselda. 'The bodies of Father Christopher and Sister Helen must be stored.'

Prior Dominic shook his head. 'We are deeply sorry to have lost two of our Order, but they died by suicide, so they cannot remain in the priory. They will not be buried in our cemetery, and it will be necessary that they are laid face down and perhaps —'

Richard interrupted him. 'It will be my duty as the coroner to instruct upon where the bodies will be buried, but you are correct that it will be in unhallowed ground. As for being laid face down or any other measures — like decapitation or being staked through the heart — they will not be considered.'

Hubert, who had been standing unobtrusively inside Mother Griselda's parlour, involuntarily reached for his arrowhead. He was aware that local practices were based upon the fear that those who self-killed had lost faith in God and could indeed have made some pact with the Devil. It was widely believed that they could rise from the grave to attack the living as they slept.

Richard went on, 'The weather is cold, so they could be placed in coffins and stored outside where their bodies will not begin to putrefy.'

Bishop Lewis stamped his foot and immediately let out a howl of pain. 'Perhaps you are missing the point, Sir Richard. We can speed matters up considerably if we simply think logically.'

'Please enlighten us, my lord,' Richard replied.

'It is obvious. These two people killed themselves because of what was brought into the priory. A demon.'

'I agree!' grunted Earl Henry. 'We witnessed it this morning. Someone desecrated the birth girdle.'

'That appears to have been Sister Helen,' Richard volunteered. He reached into his pouch and withdrew the balled piece of vellum. 'This was in her mouth and she was wearing the full habit of a nun.' He turned to Mother Griselda. 'I think you should tell everyone here what occurred in the night in the lay sisters' dormitory.'

The Mother Superior told them of the spectre who had woken the sisters by running through the dormitory and shouting that they should purge themselves.

'I did not wish to alarm our distinguished guests by informing them of this,' she added. 'My apologies. But you see, it looks as though Sister Helen, having been overcome with guilt, slashed her wrists and bled to death in the laundry.'

'And what of Father Christopher? Why did he take his own life?' the bishop asked.

'I think it was the devil's music,' Prior Dominic said. 'Fathers Barnabas and Jacob had complained to me about it. They did not feel that musical instruments should have been brought to the priory, far less played. I have to admit that I sanctioned their use by the minstrel, but I regret this decision now.'

'But what of the minstrel himself?' Isabella asked. 'He was seen having that devilish fit in front of Sister Odelina's cell. She must have been watching through that cross-shaped squint hole, which is why she suddenly screamed out as she did.'

'I am going to begin my investigation with Rupert Bisley,' said Richard.

'And I shall come with you, Sir Richard,' Prior Dominic stated firmly. 'I believe more than ever that he is the cause of all this woe.'

Mother Griselda walked with them to the church, where two of her senior nuns awaited her.

'We don't know what to do with the sisters, Mother Griselda,' said Sister Kathleen, the older of the two. 'They are all in such a state of agitation that I have never seen. They will not obey us and many have rent their clothes, discarded their habits and … and they are exposing their bodies.'

'And they are flagellating themselves openly,' added Sister Anne. 'Others will not leave the reredorter. They say they are purging themselves. And some are speaking in tongues or meowing like cats. It is as if they have forgotten how to speak English. They are frightening us.'

Leaving Mother Griselda to deal with matters, Richard, Hubert and Prior Dominic went back to the monastery, where things were equally chaotic. Brothers were running around, ignoring entreaties from the monks. Some were scuffling, others shouting obscenities, and yet others were either standing motionless or else sitting in the cloister and rocking back and forth.

They found Rupert Bisley in the hospital, tied to his cot. Some of the patients in the ward were behaving equally as strangely as the brothers in the monastery corridors.

Father Robert and Friar Simon were trying to calm them down, while a few of the most ill patients were howling in agony. Their pains seemed to have increased and become less bearable.

'I do not know what to do for them,' said Father Robert. 'No one is paying attention to me.'

'What about Master Bisley here? Why is he tied to the cot?'

'I don't know,' the minstrel answered them calmly. 'The last I knew I was in the church and felt faint when that casket was opened again. Then I vaguely recall being carried back here — to all of this!'

'We thought it best to restrain him, in case the demon rouses itself again,' Father Robert said.

'But you said you could not see a demon in me,' Rupert said evenly.

'I cannot account for anything anymore,' the monk replied. 'Yet this is the way that demons behave. They cause mischief and devastation as madness rages all around them.'

Prior Dominic nodded. 'I agree, yet I disapprove of tying him to his cot. You may release him. We must exorcise this demon as soon as we can, but first we must get our brothers and sisters back to normality.'

'I do not know how, Prior Dominic,' said Father Robert. 'I have no physic powerful enough to settle this madness that pervades the priory, nor the ability to produce enough of it.'

'I think this is beyond physic,' Prior Dominic said. 'We no longer have the birth girdle, but there is still the relic of Saint Gilbert, his blessed finger that once anointed the head of Saint Thomas. We must gather all of the brothers and the sisters in the church straight away for a special service.'

'And if any will not come, Prior Dominic?' Richard asked.

'Then my monks and Mother Superior's nuns may show them their crucifixes. Failing that, they may use their flagella. They will obey that. Meanwhile I shall inform Mother Griselda and then I will bring the finger of Saint Gilbert.'

Somehow the nuns and monks managed to herd the sisters and brothers into their respective sides of the church. However, they were not able to stop the crying and wailing, nor the aggressive and strange movements of the brothers. Fortunately, the sisters who had flagellated themselves had relinquished their whips and all were fully dressed to preserve their modesty.

Richard and Hubert accompanied Prior Dominic to his private chapel attached to his lodge, where the relic of the saint was kept locked away under the altar. It lay on a small cushion wrapped in an aged piece of linen that was heavily stained, which Richard assumed to be the blood of the saint.

In the church the senior monks were standing ready in the choir and Prior Dominic introduced Richard to them one by one.

Father Barnabas, the choirmaster, did little to conceal his irritation about the situation.

'None of this would have occurred were it not for that accursed music,' he told Richard.

'I agree with my fellow canon,' said Father Jacob, his breath smelling strongly of wine. 'That fellow should never have been sent to us. Now two of our order are dead.'

Richard ignored their comments but noted that Prior Dominic did nothing to restrain them.

'I must commend you, Sir Richard,' said Father Luke, eyeing Richard's upright posture with the ghost of a smile. 'I think your pilgrimage to Cawthorne Priory has been successful for your health.'

'And I thank you for taking care of us so well,' Richard returned. 'I enjoyed the psalms.'

Father Joseph looked miserable and anxious. 'I heard that my old friend Father Christopher's body is to be taken to Wakefield. I would rather he was laid to rest here in our cemetery, where I would be able to tend his grave until my time comes.'

'That is not possible, Father Joseph, as you well know,' said Father Dominic, kindly.

The other monks greeted Richard with either a modicum of civility or complete indifference.

Mother Griselda joined Prior Dominic on the altar steps as the prior lifted the finger upon its cushion.

'I am going to come among you, my brothers and fellow monks, and with the sacred relic of Saint Gilbert I shall point the finger at each person and bless you. Then Mother Griselda shall accompany me to the nunnery side and we shall do the same to her nuns and sisters there. You will see and feel the relief as this malady that has afflicted you all is relieved.'

Richard watched as the prior processed among the monks and brothers, holding the cushion at the level of their faces so that they could see the outline of the finger under the old blood-stained linen as he pointed it at them. And with each he made a blessing.

The effect was miraculous. As soon as the relic was directed at them they calmed, blinked and staggered, as if suddenly roused from a bad dream.

'Saint Gilbert be praised!' one called out upon recovering his old self.

It was uttered again and again until the whole of the monastery side had been treated and was now silent. The nunnery side was still a cacophony of cries and wails and animal-like noises. Prior Dominic and Mother Griselda disappeared behind the separating wall and gradually the noises diminished. The phrase 'Saint Gilbert be praised!' was echoed again and again until, finally, there was silence throughout the church.

Silence until Brother Walter began to weep copiously.

'My poor Christopher!' Richard and Hubert heard him mutter.

Lady Isabella, Bishop Lewis and Earl Henry listened as Mother Griselda and Prior Dominic described with some relief the use of the relic to subdue and bring about a recovery in all of the sisters and brothers.

'So when can we three have the same healing?' Earl Henry asked.

'Tomorrow,' the prior announced. 'The community must spend the rest of the day in prayer and giving thanks.'

'Apart from those that I need to talk to,' Richard interjected.

'And Prior Dominic and I have agreed that we shall also use the relic on the minstrel,' said Mother Griselda.

'Indeed, we shall use it on him first,' Prior Dominic concurred. 'The sooner we exorcise his demon, the safer everyone will feel.'

'And what of Sister Odelina?' Richard asked. 'Do you think it is a good idea that she remains in her anchorite cell?'

Prior Dominic looked astonished by the question. 'Yes, of course. We held a burial service with psalms from the Office of the Dead. She has left this evil world.'

'I accept that, but I will still need to talk to her.'

'There is a squint hole that you will be able to talk through,' Mother Griselda told him. 'I will tell her that you will be talking with her soon.'

'Who in the priory does talk to her?' Richard asked.

'Myself and Prior Dominic occasionally,' Mother Griselda replied. 'And Sister Patience sees to her food, her ablutions and laundry, all through a small grille. Apart from we three, no one talks directly with her.'

'Then I shall need to talk to Sister Patience as well.'

'Please take care, Sir Richard. Sister Patience is a delicate young woman. She is fearful and slow in understanding, but she is full of benevolence. She adores Sister Odelina and the feeling is reciprocated.'

Richard asked the Mother Superior and the prior to leave them for a few moments so that he could talk with the three dignitaries.

As he expected, they were reluctant to give him any information about their personal lives, as all believed themselves above answering questions from a mere sergeant-at-law. Nonetheless, he was able to confirm that Lady Isabella had indeed fallen out of favour with Queen Isabella. When gently pressed, it became clear that both she and her brother, the Bishop of Durham, had lost lands when Queen Isabella and Sir Roger Mortimer had agreed the Treaty of Northampton with Robert the Bruce, King of the Scots. And Earl Henry felt slighted that he had lost contact with King Edward, his nephew. He did not have a kind word to say about Sir Roger Mortimer.

'Did you know that the Earl of Kent had been executed?' Richard asked them.

'We did,' Lady Isabella answered for them.

'From whom did you hear this?'

'From a messenger,' she replied vaguely.

'Did this messenger tell you that the Earl of Kent's confession was read out to parliament and that he said he had been told that King Edward the Second was still alive? And also that he had been given this message by a friar who had raised a demon? That it was this demon who had told him this?'

The trio looked at each other until Earl Henry broke the silence.

'So that is what he confessed? That it was a message from a *demon?*'

'Yes, a demon raised by a friar who practised the Dark Arts.'

Bishop Lewis put a restraining hand on the earl's arm. 'Calm yourself, Henry.' Then, turning to Richard, he said, 'No, none of us had been told of any message given to the Earl of Kent.'

Richard thanked them for their time and left.

They seem perturbed that the Earl of Kent had said that a demon had sent a message, Richard thought once outside. *But they were not so surprised that such a message had been sent.*

Richard decided to question Sister Patience first, as she had discovered the dead hens and the pentagram in the hen run.

Mother Griselda arranged for the young woman to meet him in the nun's chapel attached to the nunnery chapter house. As Richard expected, the Mother Superior asked to stay in the chapel while he questioned the young sister, although she herself went to pray at the front of the chapel in order to give them some privacy.

'How long have you lived at Cawthorne Priory, Sister Patience?' Richard asked as they sat on separate pews.

'All my life, my lord.' She gave an embarrassed smile. 'It is my life to serve in any way that I can. I am so fortunate to be a lay sister and to have my duties.'

'What are those duties, Sister Patience?'

'I look after Sister Odelina's needs.'

'So I understand. And do you have a good relationship with Sister Odelina?'

'Yes, my lord.'

'Does she tell you things?'

Sister Patience looked uncertainly at the bowed figure of Mother Griselda as she prayed. She nodded.

'What sort of things?'

'I … I sometimes ask if her angel has any message for me.'

'And do they?'

'They tell her if they think I have been good and have done my duties well.'

'And do you ever tell Sister Odelina things?'

Again the young woman nodded demurely. 'I … I told her about the dead hens and that sign, my lord.'

'And what did she say?'

She told me that I must tell the nuns and sisters that she said they must purge themselves.'

'And who did you tell?'

'I told Sister Enid and the other senior nuns first, and then Mother Griselda. They … they told the nuns and the sisters.'

Richard nodded. 'I see. Now tell me, did you know Sister Odelina well before she became an anchoress?'

'Yes, my lord. We all did. She … she will be a saint one day, sir. She deserves it after all of the healing that she does — did — with her birth girdle.'

'I have heard that she was with child, but that the baby miraculously disappeared.'

Sister Patience nodded emphatically. 'I was told about it. She is a virgin, my lord. She has never … never —'

'I understand, Sister Patience. Now tell me about Sister Helen. Did you know her well?'

Tears welled in her eyes and she put a hand to her mouth to stifle a sob. 'I know all the sisters well, my lord. Sister Helen was a lovely, pure and kind sister who would do anything for anyone.'

'Did you know that she was wearing a full nun's habit when she was found in the laundry?'

'N-no, I only heard that she had … had taken her own —'

'She appears to have cut her wrists and bled to death.'

'But why would she have been wearing —?' Suddenly her eyes opened wide as she made a mental connection. 'No … no, it could not be!'

'I have heard about a nun rushing through the dormitory the other night. Do you think it could have been her?'

'I … I don't know, sir.'

'Do you recall what the nun cried out?'

'The … the same thing that Sister Odelina told me to tell the nuns to do. Purge! Purge! Purge!'

'Did you recognise the voice?'

Sister Patience shook her head, the tears now flowing copiously.

Mother Griselda talked through the squint hole to tell Sister Odelina that Richard wished to talk to her. Then, as before, she retreated to the back of the church so as not to intrude.

Richard thought it one of the oddest circumstances he had ever been called to question someone in. He stood behind the altar, peering through a tiny cross-shaped squint hole into the interior of the anchoress's cell. Although there was some light inside coming from the small overhead window, it was still dark and he could not see anything except the opposite wall, on which hung a plain wooden crucifix.

'Sister Odelina, I cannot see you,' he said after introducing himself.

'That is as I wish it,' a soft voice replied, little more than a whisper.

'Is there a reason you will not show yourself?'

'I have seen too much evil in the church and avoid seeing anyone directly.'

'That is what I wish to ask you about, Sister Odelina. The evil that you have seen.'

'I am sure that Mother Griselda or Prior Dominic or anyone else who was in the church when the sacrilege was revealed could tell you.'

'Do you mean the destruction of the birth girdle?'

'Yes, for it was the means by which a miracle was shown to the priory. It was evil that was done to it. And I saw the possession of the sisters and the brothers by the demons. And the minstrel's fit.'

'But as I understand it you knew that the minstrel, Rupert Bisley, was here to have the demon exorcised?'

'I did, but it was still odious to see the demon take him over.'

'I was in the church and heard you say that you saw fornicators present. Were there many?'

'There are many, but I cannot specifically identify them.'

'How did you see them if you cannot identify them?'

'I was told they were there by my angel. I receive many messages from my angel.'

'What form do these messages take?'

'Some come when I scry with a bowl of water and drop molten wax into it to form shapes. I can read those. Other times I am sent visions, and sometimes I hear the angel's voice.'

'Is your angel a man or a woman?'

'Neither. It is above and beyond the flesh.'

'What sort of visions do you see?'

'I see death and treachery.'

'Do you mean the deaths that have just occurred here in Cawthorne Priory?' Richard asked.

'Those and the ones before.'

'Violent deaths?'

'Natural deaths. Nuns and monks do not live forever.'

Richard could not decide whether she was being vague or deliberately evasive, but he dared not press her too much.

'Are the visions for you or are they for you to pass on to others?'

'Both. Sometimes I will pass them on to Mother Griselda. She is a nun of great goodness and wisdom.'

'What messages are you given?'

'I am told about the evil within the priory. Of the fornication and the debauchery that goes on under Mother Griselda's very nose. And also in the monastery, which Prior Dominic knows nothing of.'

'Can you be more specific about any of these messages?'

'I cannot betray my angel. And now you must go. I tire and I must pray. I have had too much contact this day with the world that I left behind.'

Richard had wanted to talk to her about Sister Patience, but he knew his time was up. He thanked her and turned to leave.

There was no reply.

Mother Griselda came to meet him when he came down the steps from the altar.

'Sister Odelina told me that she sees death, both these two and the ones before. Which ones before?'

Mother Griselda looked surprised. 'We are a community, Sir Richard. We have nuns and monks of all ages, and disease affects us as much as those in the outer world. We have lost six of our order in the past three years, but that is not unexpected. The Lord takes lives and receives souls when He decides.'

19

The pilgrim's chapel was made available for Richard to hold interviews in the monastery. After questioning the senior nuns in the nunnery, he spoke with the pilgrims, who were all surprised to learn his true identity.

Father Luke, the last to be questioned, once again expressed his own surprise when Richard spoke with him.

'I must compliment you on fooling us all, especially Father Robert, who is used to examining and treating the many people who come to his hospital.'

'It was a necessary deception, Father Luke.'

'But why, Sir Richard? We are a peace-loving community here at Cawthorne Priory. We worship together and spend our lives doing the Lord's work.'

'I anticipated that something might happen, and I needed to be here.'

'Something to do with the minstrel and his malady?'

'Perhaps.'

'Did you realise how dangerous his demon was?'

'In what way is it dangerous, Father Luke?'

The young monk smiled wryly. 'You have seen for yourself the evil that has been unleashed since his arrival: the sisters and brothers talking in tongues, purging themselves and cursing and fighting. And the fits that Master Bisley has had several times.'

'Prior Dominic said that some of the monks believe it was the minstrel's music that started the strange behaviour.'

'I like music and have my doubts about that. Yet there can be no doubt that someone has been practising the Dark Arts in the nunnery. I saw those dead hens and the pentagram painted in their blood with my own eyes. Surely an evil has been unleashed?'

'Hubert of Loxley told me that you, Father Christopher and Father Joseph held a service to cleanse the area with holy water, and that you disposed of the bodies of the hens.'

'We dared not allow any of the sisters or the brothers to become tainted by the evil.' He sighed and looked pained. 'And the fact that Father Christopher and Sister Helen most likely took their own lives proves to me that we were right to do so.'

Richard nodded. 'As you say, there is evil at work, but whether it is the result of the minstrel or his music remains to be seen.'

He said nothing about his conclusion that both deaths were murders.

Hubert and Friar Simon were waiting for Richard outside in the cold, both of them stamping their feet to keep warm.

'I heard the bell calling us to the refectory,' Richard said. 'Some sustenance would not go amiss, I must admit.'

From the rumbling of Hubert's stomach Richard could tell that his man, who had a prodigious appetite for both food and ale, agreed.

Hubert led the way, and once inside they were ushered by a brother to the head table, where the senior monks had already taken their places.

'I have little appetite for food,' grumbled Father Barnabas, 'but after all the tragedy that has befallen our beloved Cawthorne Priory, I feel I must keep body and soul together.'

'It is the truth,' agreed Father Jacob, who had already signalled for a brother with a great jug to fill his pot with ale.

Once everyone was seated, Prior Dominic took his place at the lectern to speak and read a lesson before they broke bread. He kept it short and extolled Father Christopher and Sister Helen's value to the community, avoiding any judgement concerning their mode of death.

Richard took the opportunity to question some of the senior monks. Everyone in the priory by this time was aware of Richard's position and were amenable to answering his questions, though none were verbose in their replies.

'One thing that I need to know is just how easy it is to move between the monastery and the nunnery,' he said to Prior Dominic.

'For myself it is simple. I and Mother Griselda both hold the keys to the doors into the church from the monastery and nunnery sides. When the church is not being used for a service, it is locked on both sides. So, there is no free movement between the nunnery and the monastery. The only other person who has access to the key is Sister Patience when she is attending Sister Odelina.'

'Do you ever allow anyone else to open the doors?'

'Yes, if I have sent a monk to hear confession from the nuns.'

'Hubert told me of your window house. Could someone pass between the two sides this way?'

Prior Dominic shook his head with a smile. 'The *fenestra versatilis* is designed so that only small things may be rotated from one side to the other.'

'I have seen it, my lord,' Hubert interjected. 'There is no way that anyone could pass through the device.'

'Which leads me to ask about Sister Odelina. Does this mean that she is entirely on her own, since she is walled into her cell and the church is locked between services?'

'That is so,' Prior Dominic replied. 'But the Augustinian rule is that we should observe *opus Dei*, the work of God. The nineteenth psalm says, *At Midnight I will rise to give thanks to thee.* After that we hold seven more services. The night office of Matins is followed by Lauds of the Dead, then Prime at first light, Terce three hours later, then Sext at midday and None, which we celebrate this afternoon."'

'And the nuns' Benedictine rule, is that different?'

'Not practically: we can worship together — but apart.'

After lunch, while Friar Simon went to check on Rupert in the hospital, Richard and Hubert accompanied Father Joseph to the library, where the librarian showed him the grimoire that Hubert had told him about.

'Have you studied this book?'

Father Joseph looked shocked. 'It is the work of the Devil and his followers. No, Sir Richard, it is simply a book that we feel we should own, if only to prevent others from using it.'

Richard pointed to the astrolabe on his desk. 'Do you use this a great deal?'

Father Joseph smiled. 'Actually, yes. The movement of the stars is an interest of mine. Both Father Christopher and I have been working on —' He stopped and corrected himself with a sorrowful expression. 'We were studying the skies until his vision started to deteriorate. This was his astrolabe, but after his sight deteriorated he gave it to me, knowing that I would still use it.'

'How poor was Father Christopher's vision?' Richard asked Hubert as they left the library.

'It was not good, my lord. Hence that glass he hung round his neck. I have rarely seen men squint so much — apart from

Earl Henry, who also seems to have poor sight. Mayhap he would benefit from using a glass like the one Father Christopher used.' Suddenly, he snapped his fingers. 'At the refectory the other day, when Simon and I first met him, he said that he regretted his vision was failing. He looked at one of the brothers' tables and said that he was pleased that he could leave his work to younger eyes.'

'Are you wondering whom he meant, Hubert?'

'Well, my lord, I was thinking of —'

'Of Brother Walter, who was so distraught upon finding his body.'

'Indeed, my lord.'

'Then find him and bring him to the chapel. I think it is time that I had a talk with him.'

The young lay brother was still very upset but managed to hold back his tears.

'How well did you know Father Christopher?' Richard asked kindly.

'He was like a father to me, my lord. He taught me so much.'

'About what? Scripture?'

'About artistry, my lord. He … he showed me how to draw and copy illuminations. He said he thought I had … talent.'

'Did you have any reason to think that he felt melancholic?'

Brother Walter shook his head emphatically. 'No, my lord. He was the most cheerful of men.'

'So when you found him in his cell, what did you think?'

'I didn't know what to think. I … I tried to free him, but I … I did not have the strength, so I ran to get help.'

'Should you not have been at the service yourself?'

'Yes, my lord. But I had not seen Father Christopher that morning so I … I went to find him. I was worried that he might be ill. Only … I found he had hanged himself.'

Friar Simon and Father Robert were holding Rupert Bisley down on a cot when Richard and Hubert entered the little room that he had been moved to so that he was apart from the ward of the hospital.

'This must be the fourth attack he has had today,' said Father Robert as he used a spatula to hold down the flailing minstrel's tongue.

'This one started when I told him that you were investigating the two deaths,' Friar Simon explained.

'He was irritated already, because his instruments were confiscated by order of the prior,' Father Robert said as the fit started to weaken in intensity. Slowly the spasms stopped, and the minstrel appeared to drop into a deep sleep.

'Can you make up a potion for him?' Richard asked.

'I will have to make a strong one, I think,' the hospitaller replied as he removed the spatula from Rupert's mouth. 'I will have to consult my texts and check if I have the necessary ingredients.'

'Have you thought of using mugwort, castoreum and something called *oleum cerebri humani*?' Richard asked. 'These are measures that Doctor Flynn in Wakefield thought might be needed.'

Father Robert made the sign of the cross. 'I have heard of *oleum cerebri humani*, of course, but it is not something I would ever consider using. It is made from —'

'I know, from the brain of a dead man. From one who suffered a violent death.'

Hubert cringed and reached for the arrowhead under his tunic, while Friar Simon simultaneously made the sign of the cross.

Rupert Bisley suddenly woke up and vomited.

Father Robert poured a mug of water from a jug and helped the minstrel to sit up and drink.

'Are you able to understand me, Master Bisley?' Richard asked.

Rupert blinked up at him and nodded. 'Yes, I just need a moment for my head to clear. It is always thus. But tell me, was I violent?'

Father Robert shook his head. 'You have not been violent while I have been looking after you. That at least has been an improvement, apparently.'

'My instruments? Where are they? They should be by my side. I need them.'

'Prior Dominic ordered them to be confiscated,' Father Robert replied. 'I have them in my dispensary. They are quite safe.'

'May I have them? I promise I shall not play them.'

'I should think that would be acceptable, after I have spoken with you,' Richard interceded. 'Now tell me, have you heard about what has happened in the priory?'

Rupert nodded. 'I know that I had a seizure in the church, and one of the brothers who helps Father Robert look after the patients told me that a sister and Father Christopher have taken their own lives.'

'That would be Brother Walter,' Father Robert put in.

'Did you know what happened?' Richard asked.

'Well, I felt unwell when the two nuns opened the casket and I saw it had been destroyed. When it happens it is like a veil coming over me, and then I know nothing else until I come round.'

'And what do you think brought on this last attack?' Richard queried. 'Had you just seen or heard something?'

Rupert shrugged. 'Perhaps I was just upset at hearing that two people had died.'

That evening Richard and Hubert walked round the monastery cloister as Richard recounted everything he had gleaned that day.

'So, we have two murders, one in the nunnery and one in the monastery.'

'Are they linked, my lord?'

'I think it highly likely, as both have been arranged to appear as suicide.'

'Do you think that whoever beheaded the hens and left those pentagram signs, and tore up the birth girdle, is the murderer, my lord?'

'Yes, I do, Hubert. The question is why?'

'You said earlier that the things you feared would happen have already begun. What exactly did —?'

'Hush, Hubert,' Richard whispered. 'We are not alone. There, in the shadows!'

Richard suddenly started running along the cloister, then vaulted over the low balustrade and darted across the square. Running feet could be heard from the other side.

Hubert followed and dashed through a doorway, only to hurtle into Richard, who was on his knees. They both crashed to the floor.

'Keep quiet, Hubert,' Richard said as they got to their feet. He pointed to a rope that was strung across the bottom of the door, a foot off the floor. 'That was set to trip us if we realised we were being watched and listened to. Clever, but we are too late to catch them now.'

'Do you think —?'

'Yes, and now whoever it is knows that we know. They will be even more dangerous.'

Sister Odelina sat up abruptly in the darkness.

'Odelina, I have returned.'

She gasped. 'I … I thought you had gone for good. That you were leaving me.'

'You have important work to do, Odelina. But first I must reveal myself to you.'

'I am to see you? In your angelic splendour?'

'Come to your squint hole, Odelina. Tell me when you have pressed your eye to the squint.'

She rose and crossed to the wall of the cell.

'But it is still dark. I will see nothing.'

'You will see me surrounded by light. Tell me when you are there, Odelina.'

'I am looking, but I do not see you. I see no light.'

'Purge! Purge! Purge!'

The sisters were all rudely awakened by the wailing voice. In the weak light from the candles at each end of the dormitory, all saw the veiled nun staggering between the cots, waving her blood-stained hands at them.

'Is it Sister Helen?'

'It is her ghost!'

'Heaven save us!'

As the spectral figure left the dormitory many of the wailing and crying sisters were reaching for their crucifixes. Some were reaching for the *flagella* they kept under their bedding.

'Purge! Purge! Purge!'

The brothers had returned from the Lauds service and the dormitory was full of the noise of slumbering and snoring men. It was Brother Samuel's turn to wake and rouse his fellows for the service of Terce.

With a yawn he opened his eyes, stretched his arms and after silently thanking the Lord for allowing him to sleep since Lauds when they had prayed for Father Christopher and Sister Helen, he threw back his blanket, pulled on his habit over the clothes that he wore night and day underneath it, and pushed his feet into his rope sandals.

The candles at the end of the dormitory had burned down to their last inch and threw off a dull light, so he did not notice the empty cot among the sleeping brothers.

He liked being up first because it gave him the opportunity to get his ablutions done without having to wait. Then he would return to the dormitory to rouse his fellows with a shake of each slumbering shoulder and a smile of greeting, for there would be no talking.

He made his way downstairs and past the undercroft to the latrine. As he walked, he allowed himself to hum one of the songs he had heard the minstrel sing. It had made him feel a little homesick for the old days when his mother would sing to him and his younger brothers and sisters.

Father Matthew's body was slumped across the latrine, blood dripping on the floor from the terrible slash across his throat. A knife lay in the pool of blood as if it had slipped from his hand.

Sister Patience had risen as usual and gone to the kitchen to prepare porridge, bread and water for Sister Odelina. Mother

Griselda was already up and had said her prayers when Patience knocked on her door. Together they went to the church, where Mother Griselda unlocked the door for them to enter.

Genuflecting before the altar, Mother Griselda knelt to pray while Sister Patience mounted the steps and went to the squint.

'Good morning, Sister Odelina,' she said softly. 'I have your food.'

There was no reply, but Patience was used to that and thought little of it.

Crossing to the grille at the foot of the wall, she stopped and stared in horror at the trickle of blood that had oozed through the grille.

'Mother Griselda!' she cried. 'Look!'

'What is it, my child?' the Mother Superior asked urgently. Then she too stopped when she saw blood on the wall between the two halves of the church. At the foot of it lay the body of the minstrel Rupert Bisley. There was blood on his forehead and in his right hand was a long, thin dagger. The blade was covered in blood.

20

The whole priory was in a state of uproar. The lay sisters had become hysterical and were weeping and tearing their clothes, much as they had behaved the time before. Many were speaking in tongues, the sounds incoherent and horrible to hear.

In the monastery news of Father Matthew's death had spread quickly, as Brother Samuel's screams had roused the monks and brothers even before he reached the dormitory.

Prior Dominic had unlocked the monastery side of the church to find Mother Griselda in a state of agitation herself, as she tried to comfort Sister Patience.

'He … he has the demon inside him and I think he has slain Sister Odelina, then he has tried to dash his brains out.'

Richard and Hubert had first examined the body of Father Matthew before following the commotion coming from the nunnery side of the priory. They came upon Father Dominic kneeling over the body of Rupert Bisley.

'He is still alive,' the prior said over his shoulder. 'I can feel his heart beating, but I cannot rouse him.'

Brother Walter came running into the church. 'Prior Dominic, I have ill news. The minstrel has gone from the hospital.'

The prior stood aside to reveal the body at his feet. 'He is here.'

The young brother clapped a hand to his mouth and then made the sign of the cross. 'Oh no, it is as Father Robert feared. He must have had another fit and … and…' He pointed to the long, blood-stained dagger. 'What has he done?'

Richard mounted the steps to the altar and went to look at the blood that had trickled through the grille. He knelt down and tried to see into the cell through the grille.

'I cannot see anything,' he said.

'Nor can I see anything through this tiny squint hole, my lord,' said Hubert. He put a finger into the hole and felt the stone. 'Except there is blood splattered on it. Shall we have the wall taken down?'

'No. Fetch me a looking glass and a rag first.'

Brother Stephen had been on duty at the gatehouse overnight and was unaware of the noises within the priory. He was well wrapped against the cold and the dampness of the thick mist. He was amusing himself by playing marbles when he heard the sound of horses approaching. It was highly unusual, since hardly anyone ever arrived at the priory so early in the day.

Peering out, he was surprised to see not one horse but half a dozen coming out of the mist. They did not seem to be pilgrims. One was a noble, several others appeared to be men-at-arms, and one was wearing a travelling cloak with a hood. As they approached he saw that under the cloak the traveller was dressed in the attire of a monk of the Gilbertine Order.

He hurriedly rushed out and opened the gates.

'Welcome, strangers. I am —'

The noble gestured for him to stand aside. 'Go, fellow, and bring your prior. Tell him that Sir Howard de Donville and his men have arrived, escorting the Abbot of Sempringham Priory. Bring ostlers to tend to our horses.'

The abbot dismounted from his horse and threw back the hood of his travelling cloak. 'And tell Prior Dominic that Abbot Oswald the head of the Gilbertine Order is here to inspect Cawthorne Priory after hearing of the vile things that have been happening here. Tell him that exactly.'

'I see her and I'm afraid there is no doubt. Sister Odelina is dead.'

Richard peered through the grille at the looking glass he held in his hand, which he had inserted through the grille after first wiping away the blood with a rag. 'She is lying on her back and has, I believe, been stabbed through her eye. It is a horrible sight.'

Prior Dominic's voice was shaking. 'Then we must take down the wall and tend to her body.'

'And all in the priory must be told of the evil this minstrel has done,' Mother Griselda said.

Richard rose to his feet and faced them. 'We will do neither.' He picked up the blood-covered dagger and wiped it clean with the rag. He slipped the dagger under his belt and handed the rag to Hubert, ordering him to toss it through the grille into the anchoress's cell. 'Do you recognise this type of dagger, Hubert?' he whispered.

'Yes, my lord,' Hubert replied, also in a whisper. 'It is a misericorde, a dagger used to dispatch wounded knights on the field — it is pushed through a hole in the visor of a helmet. Hardly a weapon one would expect to find in a priory.'

Richard turned to the others. 'This has been a foul murder. It is imperative that you do not mention this yet to anyone.'

Mother Griselda and Prior Dominic stared at him in astonishment. Brother Walter let out a whimper and bit the knuckle of his right hand.

'But why?' Prior Dominic asked.

'Because you can hear the tumult all through the priory already. Telling your sisters and brothers of this would only make matters worse. Besides, this man needs to be taken to the hospital.'

'But he murdered our beloved Sister Odelina,' Mother Griselda said.

'I do not believe so,' Richard said firmly. 'Nor did he kill Father Matthew.'

'Another death?' Mother Griselda said with a gasp.

Richard nodded and turned to Hubert. 'Can you and Brother Walter carry the minstrel to the hospital?' he asked, before looking to the brother. 'Are you up to it?'

Brother Walter took a deep breath and nodded.

'You must say nothing other than that he was found in the church. Just tell Father Robert that he seems to have run into a wall.'

Sister Patience was sitting on the steps, crying quietly. Mother Griselda sat beside her and put an arm about her shoulders. 'Did you hear Sir Richard, my child? You must say nothing of this.'

The young sister looked up at her with tears in her eyes. 'It can't be true, Mother Griselda. Sister Odelina was so good, so pure.'

'Come with me, Patience. We have work to do.'

The noise from both the nunnery and the monastery was becoming louder.

'We must get the monks and the nuns to try to calm the brothers and sisters,' said Prior Dominic. 'And we shall have to bring them all here and again use the relic of Saint Gilbert to calm them.'

Hubert instructed Brother Walter to hook an arm under Rupert Bisley's knees while he gently lifted his trunk. They were about to leave when Brother Stephen came rushing in, immediately followed by Abbot Oswald and Sir Howard de Donville. Behind them were several armed men.

'Prior Dominic!' the abbot exclaimed, looking at the burden Hubert and Brother Walter had between them. 'What evil has been going on here? The priory is like a madhouse, with monks and brothers screaming and running around.'

The abbot was a thin man of around forty years with prominent cheekbones and black eyebrows. Richard recognised him as having been at the assembly in Winchester, as had the man standing beside him. Both men had also been amongst Sir Roger Mortimer's adherents at the feast in the Bishop of Winchester's palace.

'I am taking charge of this priory,' the abbot went on. He pointed to the noble. 'This is Sir Howard de Donville, Lord of the Manor of Lincoln. He and his men have come on behalf of His Majesty King Edward to contain the priory.'

Richard gestured for Hubert to continue to the hospital.

Prior Dominic stared aghast. 'Your Grace, I protest.'

'I care not for your protestation. Both you and the Mother Superior have much to answer for. I have heard that there have been deaths here.'

Richard stepped forward. 'There have been deaths here and I, Sir Richard Lee, Circuit Judge of His Majesty's Northern Realm and Coroner to Wakefield and the five towns, am investigating them.'

There had been none of the usual courtesies and Sir Howard de Donville only then made a perfunctory bow of acknowledgement.

'I have heard of you, Sir Richard, and am told that you are an able sergeant-at-law. I am taking charge of the priory and intend to ensure that no one leaves. My men are in the forests and have orders that if anyone attempts to escape, they must be detained. If they resist, they will be shot.' He stared belligerently. 'You can of course continue your investigations, Sir Richard.'

'And have you also been investigating the demonic practices here?' Abbot Oswald asked coldly.

Richard wondered how they knew of the deaths and the suggestion of demonic practices.

'What demonic practices are you talking about?' he asked.

'A friar carried a message from the anchoress here in this priory, who has been practising the Dark Arts. She raised a demon and it gave her the message to give to Edmund of Woodstock, the Earl of Kent.'

Finally, this begins to make sense, Richard thought.

'It was demonic nonsense,' Sir Howard said. 'Yet the Earl of Kent believed it and committed treason against the king. For that he paid with his life.'

'The anchoress must be brought before the King's Bench and tried for witchcraft. I will need to question her. Where is her cell?'

Richard answered quickly lest either Mother Griselda or Prior Dominic should tell them what had happened. 'It is not possible today. She has been given a sleeping draught by the hospitaller. She was distraught over the death of one of the sisters.'

'Then I will wait,' the abbot replied. 'Clearly there is work to be done to exorcise the demons that have possessed the brothers and sisters here.'

'We … we were about to do so, Your Grace,' Prior Dominic returned.

'Yet I must arrest the patrons of the priory,' said Sir Howard, drawing a sealed document from inside his cloak. 'We were informed that they are the instigators of the demonic activity here. I have here a warrant for the arrests of the Bishop of Durham, the Earl of Lancaster and Lady Isabella de Vesci, signed by Sir Roger Mortimer on behalf of His Majesty King Edward. Take me to them immediately. My men will detain them.'

Prior Dominic looked to Richard for guidance.

'I think you had better do as Sir Howard requests,' he said.

'And how do you propose to calm the brothers and sisters under your respective care?' Abbot Oswald demanded of Prior Dominic and Mother Griselda.

'We will bring them all here and we shall use holy water and the finger of Saint Gilbert. It has worked before. We had planned to use it to heal our patrons and the minstrel.'

'The patrons will not receive any healing,' the abbot said curtly. 'And what is the malady that this minstrel has?'

Interesting — so they do not know about Rupert Bisley, Richard thought.

'He has the falling sickness,' Richard again interceded quickly. 'He has just injured himself in an attack, and my man and one of the brothers have taken him to the monastery hospital. I am going to go and see him now.'

'And I am going to arrest the perpetrators of this evil nest!' snapped Sir Howard de Donville.

Father Robert had examined Rupert and cleaned the blood away from his head. He had extensive bruising on the forehead and about his right eye.

'He is not conscious and I fear he has bled into his skull. I cannot rouse him and when I look into his eyes I see one pupil is larger than the other. That is a bad sign, Sir Richard.'

Friar Simon was standing on the other side of the cot along with Brother Walter.

'Is there no medicine for him, Father Robert?' Simon asked.

'It is a matter of prayer. He must have run at the wall and tried to dash his brains out.'

'That is how it looks,' Richard agreed.

Hubert caught Richard's look and understood that he was not at all convinced.

'What about the finger of Saint Gilbert?' suggested Friar Simon. 'Could we try using it to heal him?'

'It would be worth trying,' replied the hospitaller.

'I agree,' said Richard. 'I shall see Prior Dominic and get it now.'

Prior Dominic was feeling pressure such as he had never felt before. Abbot Oswald stuck close to him as if he was his shadow, listening intently as he instructed the monks to bring the brothers to the church, just as Mother Griselda was doing with the nuns in the nunnery.

Richard caught up with them as they headed for the library. The abbot seemed to know about the grimoire.

He seems well informed, Richard thought. *Too well informed.*

'Prior Dominic, a word if I may,' Richard said at the door of the library, which Father Joseph had opened upon hearing them approach. 'You must carry on as best you can,' he whispered, drawing the prior to one side as the abbot entered the library with Father Joseph. 'Do not give the abbot any details about the three deaths.'

'I have instructed Father Luke to have Father Matthew's body taken from the latrine and laid out respectfully in his own cell. Father Luke will clean the blood away.'

'Rupert Bisley cannot be roused. I must take the finger of Saint Gilbert and we shall try to revive him with it.'

'No! It is a holy relic. Only —'

'There is no time to argue, Prior. Tell me where it is and where to find it. I will bring it to the church when you have assembled all the brothers and sisters.'

The prior delved under his habit and drew out four keys on a ring. 'The two large keys are for the church doors. This black one is for my private chapel, which is attached to my lodge. The more intricate one is for a small reliquary chest that you will find underneath the altar. The relic lies on a cushion within. But it must not be handled.'

'I understand. It must be left on the cushion under the linen and pointed at the person. I saw you do this.'

'Prior Dominic, come here! I need you to explain this!' cried out the abbot from the library.

'You must go, as must I,' Richard returned.

21

Returning to the little room in the hospital, Richard unlocked the small chest and took out the cushion and the linen-wrapped relic.

'Prior Dominic explained that I must point it at the minstrel. If it is going to work, then it should do so soon.'

'It will, I have no doubt,' Friar Simon said eagerly. 'Just as it exorcised the demons from the brothers and sisters last time.'

Father Robert stood watching as Richard pointed the cushion at the unconscious minstrel's head. As he did so, both Father Robert and Friar Simon started to pray. Brother Walter clasped his hands together and screwed his eyes tightly shut.

They watched and waited, but nothing happened. Rupert Bisley's breathing continued, but he made no movement otherwise.

After some minutes Richard replaced the relic and cushion in the chest and locked it again.

'At the minstrel's trial in Wakefield, Doctor Flynn was doubtful that exorcism would work and thought instead that trephination would be needed,' said Richard.

'That is barbarism,' said Friar Simon.

'Yet I think in this case, it may be necessary,' said Father Robert. He lifted Rupert's hand and when he let it go, it flopped heavily onto the bed. 'See, there is no power in him.'

'Do you know how to perform this operation?' Richard asked.

'I have the surgical instruments and did it once many years ago. It was for a brother who is now one of the monks. Or I should say was, for it was for Father Matthew after he had a fall in the winter snow.'

When Father Robert gathered the instruments that he needed for the procedure, Richard signalled for Hubert to join him outside.

'You are not convinced that Rupert did this to himself, are you, my lord?' Hubert said.

'No, and nor am I convinced that he murdered Sister Odelina. But I need to hear it from his own lips. That is why it is so important that we try Doctor Flynn's approach and get Father Robert to open his head.'

'Why did you try the relic, my lord?'

'I needed to be able to try it myself. But listen, for time is of the essence. There have been four murders and yet there could be even greater tragedy. I had not expected the abbot and Sir Howard de Donville to appear and take over, yet now that they have we must act. Sir Howard has said that no one can leave the priory.'

'And if they resist arrest they will be shot. I heard him say that, my lord.'

'If it was not so desperate I would not ask you, Hubert, but will you go to Sandal Castle and ask Sir Thomas to send men?'

'I will, my lord. Fortunately there is mist. I had better sneak out on foot, go to the village and get a horse there.'

'Godspeed, Hubert, my friend. I think the lives of many depend on us.'

When Richard returned, he dismissed Friar Simon and Brother Walter from the room. 'Perhaps I can help,' he told the hospitaller. 'I have seen many wounds in battle and blood does not make me squeamish.'

Nodding acknowledgement and using scissors to cut hair from an area of the minstrel's scalp, Father Robert then picked up a small scalpel.

'How do you know where the bleed is?' Richard asked.

'I am not sure at all,' Father Robert returned, 'but the pupil of his eye is smaller on this side where he has the most bruising, so I suspect it is this side of his brain that is affected.'

He made an oval-shaped incision in the scalp, then worked quickly to lift the flap of skin.

He used a clean rag to wipe away the blood then handed it to Richard. 'Just dab any blood vessels that ooze. I have to see what I am doing and my hands are going to be occupied.'

Picking up a tubular instrument with serrations around its edge, he placed the cutting edge against the bone and began to work it back and forth as quickly as he could. He had to press hard to start the process, but gradually the serrations cut into the minstrel's skull with a rasping noise. As he built up the speed of his sawing, the friction on the bone caused wisps of smoke to rise from the site, not unlike when rubbing sticks to make fire.

An odour of blood and smoke filled the air.

'I'm almost through, so I have to be careful now,' he said softly as Richard swabbed more blood away from the site. 'I don't want to go through into his actual brain or I could kill him.'

There was a sudden give under his hand. 'Almost there.' He pointed to a pair of fine tongs he had placed in readiness. 'Can you hand me those, Sir Richard? I need to just lift this small disc of bone.'

And as he did so there was a sudden spurt of blood. 'Thanks be to the Lord!' he breathed. 'I was right; there is a collection of blood here.'

Then, working with the tongs and a small scalpel, he made the hole in the membrane that covered the grey-pink brain slightly larger so that the blood oozed out to collect in a small wooden bowl he placed in readiness. He waited until no more came out, then he replaced the disc of bone and the scalp flap.

'Now we just have to wait and hope. If he comes round all right, then I'll stitch his scalp back later.'

To their amazement, Rupert Bisley stirred just two minutes later. Not long after that his eyes fluttered open and he tried to sit up. Father Robert held him down.

'Stay calm, Master Bisley,' the monk said. 'You have had a bad head wound and you need to lie still.'

Rupert's eyes fluttered and closed.

Father Robert turned to Richard. 'He must sleep now, Sir Richard.'

'And I must get the relic to Prior Dominic in the church. Then I shall return and ask the minstrel some important questions.'

Sir Howard de Donville stared contemptuously at the three patrons of Cawthorne Priory. They had reacted with anger upon hearing him read out the warrant for their arrests.

'It is nonsense,' barked the Earl of Lancaster. 'I am King Edward the Second's cousin, and I was head of the regency council for King Edward his son who now sits upon the throne.'

'So, cousin to a dead monarch and no longer head of a regency council,' de Donville retorted.

'This is an outrage! I am a friend to Queen Isabella,' snapped Lady Isabella.

'But friend no more, my lady. You were banished from court and have been caught plotting against the king.'

The bishop rose to his feet and winced. 'I shall have you excommunicated, you insolent dog.'

Sir Howard de Donville started to laugh. 'I care not for any of your protests. The charges are clear; you three have been plotting against the king and instigated the practice of the Dark Arts here. The Abbot of Sempringham himself is investigating this and has taken charge of the priory after the necromancing anchoress of yours released demons that have possessed all of the brothers and sisters. So I repeat, you are all under arrest and will be taken to London for trial before the King's Bench. In case you didn't understand the warrant, it is by order of Sir Roger Mortimer, the Earl of March and Queen Isabella on behalf of His Majesty. You will remain here under the eyes of my armed guards.'

He left the room and the door was locked.

'It is what we feared,' said Lady Isabella. 'We are undone.'

It had not been easy, but with a mixture of cajoling, threatening and with some actual physical manhandling the nuns and the monks had again managed to get the sisters and brothers into the church, where Prior Dominic and Mother Griselda were waiting in front of the altar along with Abbot

Oswald.

As before there was much noise, a cacophony of wailing and meowing noises as few seemed to stand steady at ease.

Richard hurried in with the reliquary chest. 'It had no effect upon the minstrel,' he told Prior Dominic and Mother Griselda quietly. 'But Father Robert has opened his skull and let the blood inside his head out. He sleeps now.'

'Waste no more time, Prior Dominic,' snapped the abbot. 'You must exorcise these demons, and then I shall order them all to do suitable penance. You and the Mother Superior can then prepare yourselves to be banished from the order.'

Prior Dominic tightened his lips and Mother Griselda lowered her head, but neither said anything. Richard watched as Prior Dominic opened the reliquary and took out the cushion and the blood-stained bundle covering the relic.

As he had done before, Prior Dominic announced what he was about to do and then he went among the monks and brothers, pointing the cushion at their faces and muttering a blessing in Latin each time. And just as before, the effect was almost instantaneous. The posturing, strange noises and movements all subsided, and those affected seemed to wake up as if from a nightmare. They all crossed themselves and thanked the Lord and Saint Gilbert.

Then Prior Dominic and Mother Superior went into the nunnery side of the church and repeated the whole process under the stern observation of Abbot Oswald.

When all was done, they returned to the altar where Abbot Oswald announced to the church that he had assumed charge of the priory. There were looks of astonishment and sorrow, but under his blazing eyes and stern voice no one dared to say anything.

Like beaten dogs, Prior Dominic and the Mother Superior left the church together to return the reliquary to the prior's chapel.

Richard watched them go and then hurried back to the hospital.

Hubert had gone to the gatehouse where Brother Stephen had again taken up his position. From there Hubert looked out through the grille to see if there were signs of Sir Howard de Donville's men close by the walls. Visibility in the mist was poor and he estimated he could only see for about twenty-five paces, so there could be men waiting nearby.

'But sir, Sir Howard and Abbot Oswald said that no one was to leave the priory. I am not permitted to open the gate,' Brother Stephen said plaintively.

Hubert grinned and patted him on the shoulder. 'Have no fear, Brother. I'm not planning on using the gate.'

Leaving the gatehouse, he kept to the wall and walked round to the point where he felt he could best reach the woods through the mist.

Unbuckling his sword belt, he reached up and placed his weapon on top of the wall. Then, hoisting his travelling cloak up, he nimbly climbed and swung over the wall and let himself down noiselessly.

'So far, so good,' he whispered to himself as he made his way into the thick mist.

'Well?' Father Robert asked as Richard returned to the hospital room where the hospitaller was watching over the sleeping minstrel. 'Is all well?'

Richard nodded. 'The brothers and sisters all responded to the finger of Saint Gilbert. But I am afraid that the abbot has said that your Prior and Mother Griselda are to be banished from your order.'

'In the Lord's name, why? It makes no sense.'

'Because of the demons he says they have unleashed.'

'But if any demon was unleashed, it was from Master Bisley here.'

'I should tell you this, Father Robert. Sister Odelina is dead. And it looked as if Rupert Bisley had stabbed her through the squint hole.' Richard looked down at the sleeping man. 'You can open your eyes now, Rupert Bisley. I am sure you are feigning sleep, just as you have feigned all of these fits.'

Rupert opened his eyes, which immediately filled with tears. 'The anchoress is dead?' he asked.

'She is, and it was made to look as if you had killed her with a long dagger called a misericorde.'

'It was not me. I … I failed to protect her. I tried to grab the killer, but after a tussle he threw me against the wall. I … I don't remember anything else.' His hand went to his head. 'Now I have this pain that is stopping me from thinking properly.'

Father Robert looked at them both in disbelief. 'I do not understand.'

'I know that you are not the killer, Rupert Bisley,' said Richard. 'But you know who is.'

'I do, but I only had my suspicions until I finally heard the voice. I sneaked out of the hospital last night and heard them talking to the anchoress through the wall. I didn't know what was planned until I saw that long dagger suddenly drawn, then I charged. But I was too late.'

'Who was it?' Richard demanded.

Prior Dominic placed the reliquary chest beneath the altar in his private chapel then stood and turned to face Mother Griselda.

She threw herself into his arms and they kissed. Not their usual passionate kissing, but this time chaste and loving.

'Our world has crumbled, Dominic, and we are cursed. We will go to Hell and be eternally damned.'

'Who knows what fate holds for Lady Isabella, the earl and Bishop Lewis?' he replied.

Hubert started to run on the balls of his feet, having come across no one. He was beginning to wonder if there were any soldiers other than those who had entered the priory with Sir Howard de Donville and the Abbot of Sempringham.

Then he ran straight into a man. The fellow stumbled and fell. From the sound Hubert could tell that he was wearing chainmail.

'I have one of them!' the man shouted. 'Here —'

He said no more as Hubert struck him full in the face, knocking a tooth out in the process and rendering him unconscious.

He stood for a moment as he heard running footsteps coming towards him from different directions. Worse, he heard the unmistakeable sound of swords being drawn from sheaths.

He drew his own and dropped into a fighting pose, ready for them.

They came at him from three sides with swords raised.

'Drop that sword!' one barked at him. 'We have orders to detain anyone trying to leave the priory. Resist and you're a dead man.'

'Only three of you,' Hubert countered. 'Step aside and you may live beyond this day.'

They cursed him and attacked as one. Hubert drew his dagger and parried one blow with his sword and another with the dagger. He was too fast for the third attacker and delivered a cutting blow to his leg. Then he smashed the pommel of his sword into the face of the first and slashed the other's wrist so that his sword fell.

Having disabled all three, he was choosing which direction to take next when another voice called out.

'Stand or die on that spot of earth!'

Hubert saw a man step out of the mist towards him, a longbow raised and a primed arrow aimed directly at his chest.

22

Prior Dominic and Mother Griselda spun round in unison.

'A touching scene! And soon to be your last.'

'Luke? What do you mean?' Mother Griselda asked.

Father Luke had closed the door behind him and crept slowly up the short aisle of the chapel. 'It is almost over. Everything has worked out to perfection, as I knew it would. My new master will be pleased.'

'Your new master?' Prior Dominic repeated. 'You … you mean that you have betrayed us?'

Father Luke laughed. 'Of course I have betrayed you, you pair of fornicating hypocrites. I know that I am your son. And I take it the dim-witted Patience is your daughter, my sister?'

'You were twins. I carried and gave birth to you in secret, when the other nuns thought I was ill. Only Sister Elfreda knew.'

'And poor benighted Odelina was so stupid and in love with you. I suppose she noticed your belly getting bigger and convinced herself that she was pregnant, too.'

'It was a miracle, Luke,' Griselda said.

'Hogwash! She was a gullible fool, just as I was until I worked out who I was and why you both paid me special attention. You groomed me for deception, only you didn't know it.'

'We have loved you both, but at a distance as our circumstances dictated,' Prior Dominic said.

'And I hated you. I hate this priory and everything that you stand for. That's why I became Odelina's angel. It was so much easier when she had herself walled up, but that too was at my suggestion.'

'You? You gave her the message that King Edward was still alive?' The prior stared in disbelief.

'I did. A wonderful lie that I made up. And I had fun dressing as a nun so I could seduce Sister Helen, just as I seduced Christopher. They both had to die, of course. Helen because she could expose me and Christopher for the same reason, and also because he realised I had hurt my hand by getting splinters in it when I painted that pentagram on the hen house. Strangling him was the easy part. He didn't suspect anything as I embraced him as a lover, and the killing was swiftly done. I then lay his body on his desk, threaded a rope through that eyeglass cord of his, which I tightened round his neck, and tossed the rope over the beam. Standing on the stool, I then hoisted him up until his body was upright, as if standing on the desk. Then I swiftly tossed the end of the rope over the beam again, so I could knot it to hold him secure. All I had to do then was shove his feet off the desk and upend the stool to make it look as if he had hanged himself.'

A cruel, smug smile spread across his lips. 'Oh, and Matthew had to go in case he told you that I had been to London at the same time as him, but on a different mission.'

He chuckled again. 'And you — on behalf of the pompous Lady Isabella and her brother and old Wryneck Henry — sent me to London to give the message that I had invented to the Earl of Kent. I did give it to him, of course, but I also made myself known to Sir Roger Mortimer and told him everything. What a wonderful web we spun. Sir Roger gets rid of his enemies by this ploy, including that ridiculous drunken criminal who beheaded Woodstock. Sir Roger gave me the task of despatching him after the execution in case Woodstock said anything to him before he struck with the axe. He did not want to risk the drunken oaf telling people of the earl's final words, especially if there was anything that could put Woodstock in a good light or cast Sir Roger as a villain. He could have even concocted some tale of his own. I enjoyed severing his head and putting it on my own spike outside Winchester Castle.'

There was the sound of clapping behind him, and he turned on his heel to see Richard standing at the door.

'Thank you for explaining all, *Father Luke*!'

The monk laughed slyly. 'Ah, so our pilgrim, or is it our judge, has joined us, to witness the end of this little play.' He drew a small flask out of his habit and tossed it to Prior Dominic. 'It is poison of the very finest. Drink it, both of you, and be spared from being burned as witches as you assuredly will be after I tell my tale.'

'You have forgotten about me,' Richard said.

'Not at all. I have only to shout and Sir Howard's armed men will come in, and with a word from me they will slay you. Did you not think their arrival on this very day was strange? Well, it was as we planned. I arranged the deaths, I scared the sisters and brothers witless, and I executed the witch Odelina. She would have been burned anyway, so out of kindness I despatched her to find happiness with her angel!'

Luke clicked his tongue. 'That damned fool of a minstrel made it even easier for me when the whole priory was prattling on about his demon. I saw the opportunity here and played on that.'

'And what of Sir Ranulf Fermont? Why did you murder him and his servant?'

'He showed himself to have no love for my master at the feast in Winchester. I was there, you know, but you did not recognise me.'

So it was him I saw at the palace, Richard thought. *He was the provocative long-haired young man dressed in a simple brown tunic sitting opposite Ranulf.*

'I had baited him. It was easy. And it was important to prevent the Lincoln judge from trying to impede our friends from Lincolnshire, Sir Howard de Donville and the Abbot of Sempringham. They had merely to arrive here today with their warrant and find that I had done the rest. Sir Roger did not want to risk him interfering once he returned to Lincolnshire, so he commanded me to kill him and his servant. I must admit that the old fool irritated me with that cow horn, so I used it to send him to his maker, after I slit his servant's throat.'

'I am damned for bringing you into the world!' Mother Griselda said bitterly as she tried to snatch the flask from the prior.

'No, it is me that has sinned beyond redemption,' said Prior Dominic, unstopping the flask. He raised it to his lips and in one smooth move appeared to drain it.

'Good, it will not take long,' the monk said with a sneer. 'But what will you do now, Mother? Will you open your wrists and escape the stake? Or shall I do it for you, as I did with Sister Helen after I throttled her?'

Prior Dominic groaned and doubled up, then fell to the floor.

'Dominic, my love!' Griselda cried, dropping to her knees and cradling his head in her lap.

'And now, pilgrim, I just need to deal with you,' the monk said, pulling a sword from beneath his habit.

Hubert stared at the bowman.

'You better fire true, my friend, because you will only have one chance,' he said. 'Then I mean to break your neck.'

'I never miss,' the man returned.

Hubert braced himself as he heard the twang and the whooshing noise of an arrow in flight. An arrowhead went right through the man's neck and blood spurted out as he tumbled forward, the bow falling from his hands as fell.

Hubert stared in disbelief as a knight emerged from the mist with his longbow in his hand. 'I had no choice but to kill him,' he said. 'You are Sir Richard Lee's man, are you not? I am Sir William de Bohun, one of King Edward's retinue. I was a pilgrim like Sir Richard, until he revealed himself when the body of that monk was found hanging. He sent me to get aid.'

'I am so skilled at killing, but I do not believe that I have run a man through before,' the killer said as he advanced on Richard.

He lunged, but Richard dodged adroitly. Drawing the long, thin misericorde dagger, he stabbed it through Father Luke's arm, causing him to drop the sword. Before he could cry out in pain, Richard drove his other fist into the monk's face, breaking his nose and sending his head crashing backwards onto the altar step.

Richard put his finger to his lips. 'Try not to make a sound, Mother Griselda,' he whispered. 'I must check for men-at-arms outside.'

He eased the door open and peered out.

From somewhere nearby, a horn was blown and then a voice that he recognised boomed out.

'Drop your weapons, you curs! I am Sir Thomas Deyville, the Steward of Sandal Castle, and I and my men have possession of this priory.'

'Sir Richard,' Mother Griselda beseeched. 'Help me, if you will.'

He turned to see Father Dominic getting to his feet with the Mother Superior's aid. 'I only pretended to drink the poison so as to gain an opportunity to assist you,' he said.

The Abbot of Sempringham looked on the verge of an apoplectic attack and Sir Howard de Donville had a face like thunder as Richard, his father-in-law Sir Thomas and Sir William de Bohun confronted them.

'Your whole nefarious plot is known and His Majesty King Edward will be made aware of it, and of your master's part in it.'

'I am leaving and taking my prisoners with me,' Sir Howard said challengingly.

'You can leave with your men, but not with their weapons,' said Sir William. 'And not with the distinguished patrons of this priory.'

'I have a warrant!'

'And I have one from His Majesty the king himself,' retorted Sir William de Bohun. 'It countermands any authority I may come against.'

Later, after Sir Thomas and Sir William had despatched the abbot and Sir Howard and their men, Richard returned to the hospital with Hubert.

Richard told Rupert Bisley of what had happened.

'I had suspected that you were not having real fits, and I was never convinced about a demon. I also didn't believe that a relic could cure the falling sickness.'

'But you saw how powerful the finger of Saint Gilbert was,' offered Father Robert.

'I did not, because I have the finger in my purse, so I knew that to be a delusion. What everyone thought to be the relic was in fact the key to the prior's chapel. It had no power over a demon. It seems that believing it was real was sufficient, as I thought it would be, hence my little deception when I went to get it from the prior's chapel.'

He turned again to the minstrel. 'So tell me, who are you and why did you come to Cawthorne Priory?'

'I came for vengeance, Sir Richard. Sir Roger Mortimer had my father murdered four years ago. You see, I am the bastard son of Edmund Fitzalan, the Earl of Arundel and of Sister Honoraria, who was a nun at Arundel Priory. Mortimer and Queen Isabella had my father executed alongside Sir Thomas de Micheldever and Sir John Daniel without trial. I had been in his party when he tried to escape, and I was sent to tell his wife that he had to flee. But I could not reach her, as enemy soldiers were everywhere. So I made my way to Hereford, where I witnessed his brutal beheading. I vowed vengeance upon Mortimer then and there. I have musical skills so put myself in a position to be employed by the Bishop of Winchester as a minstrel, for I knew that eventually Mortimer would arrive there. And he did, along with all his lackeys — men who had abused my father and his friends.

'I killed Sir Jasper de Beausale at the feast that you attended at the bishop's palace, Sir Richard. I dropped a pellet of poison from my shawm into his wine from the minstrel's gallery. He had a fit and died.'

Richard nodded. 'Indeed, I remember that well. The feast was called off.'

'Well, I knew my way about the palace and I kept a watch on Mortimer. He would go to pray in the bishop's chapel and one night I was there ready to stab him to death, but then another came and I heard them plotting. When I heard that there was an anchoress that had to be slain, I stayed my hand. The plan was to incriminate the Earl of Lancaster, who was the only hope for our England. I determined that I must go there and prevent this killer from carrying out the plot.' Rupert sighed and let out a sob. 'But I did not know who he was, for I did not see his face. I only knew his voice.'

'As you told me,' said Richard.

'But I failed. Just as I failed the memory of my father. And now I must face justice for my crimes.'

Richard patted his shoulder. 'I think you achieved more than you give yourself credit for. The earl is safe, and although I saw a person die from a fit at a feast I attended, there is no suggestion that he was killed by any hand.'

Hubert looked puzzled. 'But does this mean that Friar Simon was involved, my lord? It was he who suggested that Rupert should be sent to Cawthorne Priory.'

'That was me again,' Rupert said. 'When I reached Wakefield, I joined the troupe of tumblers and jongleurs and started to spin the tale about my non-existent malady. We would drink in the taverns in the towns we entertained in. In The Bucket Inn, Friar Simon regaled the drinkers about the amazing cures performed by the anchoress at Cawthorne, in exchange for having drinks bought for him. I knew then that Cawthorne Priory was the religious house the killer would be making for. I had to get myself there by pretending to have the falling sickness, and then wait until I could identify him. It was not easy, since the monks and brothers rarely spoke, but once I heard Father Luke talking I knew it was he. He did not recognise me in my ordinary clothes. I made sure that he saw me arrested and saw my eyes, which burned red after I had rubbed salt into them.'

'So he would think you were possessed by a demon?' asked Hubert.

Richard nodded. 'Since you put up no objection about being sent to Cawthorne Priory, I suspected this had to be the place that Sir Roger Mortimer and Queen Isabella wanted me to find their mysterious friar. And when Sir William de Bohun came to me and informed me that he had visited Sir Ranulf's sister, then warned Lady Isabella de Vesci and her brother the Bishop of Durham, and Earl Henry, it became clearer. There was a plot to incriminate them in some treasonous undertaking. Since they were known to be patrons of Cawthorne Priory, it had to be here. Which is why two pilgrims arrived here shortly after you did. They were Sir Richard and Sir William, both in disguise, though neither was known to the other at first.'

Richard and Hubert returned to the guest house, where Richard's father-in-law was enjoying a mug of ale with Sir William de Bohun.

'Should you be supping ale, Sir Thomas?' Richard asked. 'Remember your podagra.'

His father-in-law guffawed cheerily. 'Pah! I have never felt so well, Richard. That brew that Doctor Flynn gave me cured me completely when I took enough of it. And this sortie that my young fiend Sir William here brought me on has been the finest medicine I could hope for. It has cured my melancholy.'

'I am grateful to you both, my lords,' Hubert said. 'I thought that I was about to breathe my last out there in the mist.'

'We couldn't allow a good fighting man like yourself to be wasted,' said Sir William. 'I saw you take on three armed men. His Majesty King Edward has need of stout friends and good fighters like you.'

Sir William de Bohun explained how he had been despatched as a messenger by Sir William de Montagu following his late-night meeting with Richard at Winchester. The king's friends felt it important to warn the Earl of Lancaster and Lady de Vesci that after the Earl of Kent's execution, all attention would be directed upon them by Mortimer and Queen Isabella.

'I realised when we visited Sir Ranulf's sister that two messengers had visited her before Hubert and myself,' explained Richard.

'I was one,' said Sir William, sipping his ale.

'And the other was the king's messenger,' said Richard.

'I duly warned them all, including Archbishop Melton in York, and then Sir Richard made himself known to me.'

Richard went on, 'So there I was, having been taken into Sir Roger Mortimer's confidence, on some nebulous plea to keep my eyes open and to report anything suspicious about priories or monks. Simultaneously, Sir William de Montagu told me that the king needed friends. When the minstrel Rupert Bisley appeared in my court, I wondered whether this might be the thread that I should follow. Hence I became a pilgrim.'

'What will happen now, my lord?' Hubert asked. 'I mean to the prior and Mother Superior and that villain, Father Luke?'

'I think that Sister Odelina will be entombed properly in her cell. Mother Griselda and Prior Dominic will either face Canon Law or just disappear and live in penitence together for the rest of their lives. I certainly have no intention of holding them. As for Father Luke, I imagine he is going to face eternal damnation, as indeed he should. His journey there, however, is unlikely to be without pain.'

HISTORICAL NOTES

The Minstrel's Malady is a work of fiction, which continues the adventures of Sir Richard Lee and his assistant Hubert of Loxley. The first three books in the series were all set towards the end of King Edward II's turbulent reign, while this novel is set at the start of his son King Edward III's reign.

King Edward II was captured by the forces of his wife, Queen Isabella and her lover Roger Mortimer, Lord of Wigmore and Earl of March on 16th November 1326. They also had his favourite, Hugh Despenser the Elder, executed in October 1326 and his son, Hugh Despenser the Younger, in November 1326.

The king was deposed in favour of his son, King Edward III, in February 1327. Allegedly, and as depicted in Kit Marlowe's play, *Edward II*, he was murdered most cruelly in Berkeley Castle in September 1327.

There is, however, much debate among historians about the veracity of King Edward II's death. *The Fieschi Letter*, written to King Edward III in around 1337 by Manuele Fieschi, a Genoese priest, avers that King Edward II was not murdered but escaped and spent the rest of his life in exile in Europe.

There are compelling arguments on both sides, which make for a most fascinating study. Indeed, the fate of King Edward II ranks alongside the fate of the Princes in the Tower among historical mysteries.

The plot for this novel gradually evolved from this mystery. Another strand comes from the case of the Nun of Watton, who lived a couple of centuries before this tale was set. She was a nun in Watton Priory, which was a Gilbertine religious house in the East Riding of Yorkshire. As explained in the novel, the order was established by Saint Gilbert of Sempringham in Lincolnshire, as the only English religious order. It permitted nuns and monks to live in the same priory, albeit separated. They could come together to worship, yet were separated by a wall in the church.

Cawthorne Priory is a fictitious Gilbertine Priory set near present-day Cawthorne village in South Yorkshire. It is, however, based on the structure of the ruins of Watton Priory.

The Nun of Watton conceived and allegedly gave birth to a baby that was taken immediately to heaven by angels, leaving no trace of pregnancy or labour. The case was recorded by Saint Aelred of Rievaulx Abbey in 1160, in which, after consultation with Gilbert, it was declared a miracle. Those interested will find much information about the case, which had a far more sinister side to it, for the brother accused of being the child's father endured a barbaric castration.

There are numerous instances of false pregnancy throughout history. The medical name for it is *pseudocyesis*. It can affect both women and men. The case of the Nun of Watton could have been mundane in that a child was delivered and then taken away and evidence of pregnancy and labour suppressed. There was, after all, considerable benefit to be gained in having had a miracle declared in a religious house.

Yet the idea of *pseudocyesis* or false pregnancy is also plausible. It is in essence the physical symptom of what is termed in psychiatry an *hysterical conversion*. That is, the unconscious mind produces physical symptoms in an individual in order to solve some problem or difficulty in their life. In other words, people can become convinced that they are pregnant and produce all of the symptoms of having a baby, except without one being present.

Likewise mass hysteria, the phenomenon where a group of people are affected en masse, is exhibited in another influential case that influenced the genesis of this story. In particular, the case of the Nuns of Loudon. This occurred in 1634 in the French town of Loudon, when the nuns of a local convent claimed to have been seduced by the local priest. Because of their alleged sexual relations, they perceived that they had become possessed by the Devil. They would howl like dogs, meow like cats and jump about like all manner of creatures. They claimed to be visited by demonic creatures, ghostly skeletons that walked in the convent corridors, and a black bull that appeared in their refectory. They became immodest, suffered from convulsions, and behaved with extreme lewdness.

The priest, Urbain Grandier, was brought to trial for practising witchcraft, tortured and condemned to death by burning at the stake. Throughout it all, he refused to confess or admit to any wrongdoing.

However, the possessions continued for three years after his death and many public exorcisms were made.

Some historians claim that Urbain Grandier was a victim of political persecution, for he had been critical of Cardinal Richelieu (of *The Three Musketeers* fame) in a book he had written.

The epoch of history that this novel is set in was brutal. No one's life was safe, and summary executions such as that of Edmund Fitzalan, the Earl of Arundel were not uncommon. His execution is said to have been as horrific as depicted in the prologue. What actually happened to his executioner, the latrine cleaner and condemned prisoner, is unknown, yet it is known that he performed the deed.

Sir Roger Mortimer, the Earl of March did indeed have an adulterous affair with Queen Isabella and he is known in history as the epitome of a traitor. He was the de facto ruler of England while Edward III was still a minor, but he came to grief when King Edward and a small group of his friends, notably Sir William de Montagu, William de Bohun, John Neville and others staged a swashbuckling coup at Nottingham Castle on 19th October 1330, when they arrested Mortimer and placed Queen Isabella under house arrest.

Henry, the Earl of Lancaster, who was known as Wryneck and did indeed go blind in 1330, was instrumental in this and persuaded King Edward not to summarily execute Mortimer, but to allow him a trial, albeit one in which he was not permitted to speak. He was found guilty of high treason and hanged at Tyburn in London like a common criminal on 29th November. Mortimer confessed that he had procured the death of Edmund of Woodstock, the Earl of Kent.

The confession of Edmund of Woodstock is much as indicated in this book, aside from a little poetic licence. He did confess that a friar had raised the Devil and that it had told him that King Edward II still lived.

It is also worth saying a little about relics. Birth girdles were used in medieval days as an aid to safe labour, an illustration of the belief in the divine and the protection of the saints. So too were relics of the saints, which were believed to have curative properties. My use of Sir Richard's substitution of a key for a holy relic was something that actually happened when an investigator wanted to prove that it was belief rather than a relic that was responsible for curing someone of an hysterical condition.

Finally, epilepsy was called the falling sickness in the medieval era and was considered to be caused by either a disorder of the body's humoral balance or possession by demons. Treatment of convulsion did involve holding the tongue down in the erroneous belief that the sufferer could swallow their own tongue. This is anatomically impossible and should never be done, as placing something in the mouth of someone having a seizure can be dangerous. Nowadays creating a safe place, putting the individual into a safe position and not interfering unless using suitable drugs is the correct management. This is far more effective than the gruesome *oleum cerebri humani*, which actually was advocated.

Trephination was frequently performed, in the belief that it could relieve pressure from bleeds and humoral imbalance, and release demons.

I have found many fine books useful in my research for this novel, especially the following:

Paul Doherty, *Isabella and the Strange Death of Edward II*

Aldous Huxley, *The Devils of Loudon*

Ian Mortimer, *The Greatest Traitor: The life of Sir Roger Mortimer, Ruler of England 1327–1330*

Kathryn Warner, *Long Live the King: The Mysterious Fate of King Edward II*

Alison Weir, *Isabella: She Wolf of France, Queen of England*

A NOTE TO THE READER

Dear Reader,

If you have enjoyed the novel enough to leave a review on **Amazon** and **Goodreads**, then I would be truly grateful. I love to hear from readers, so if you would like to contact me, please do so through my **Facebook** page or send me a message through **Twitter**. You can also see my latest news on my **website**.

Keith Moray

keithmorayauthor.com

Sapere Books is an exciting new publisher of brilliant fiction and popular history.

To find out more about our latest releases and our monthly bargain books visit our website: **saperebooks.com**

www.ingramcontent.com/pod-product-compliance
Lightning Source LLC
Chambersburg PA
CBHW051506030726
47592CB00006B/2129